No Trace

Robin Gilford

Alison

With best wishes,

Robin Galford.

Dec. 2021

Acknowledgements

My grateful thanks to Margaret, Sue and Ian for all their help and advice with this book.

Preface Book One

Set in the current time and on the North Cornwall coast, Emilia is horrified to stumble over what feels like a human body part in the darkness of her shed late in October. Or did she imagine the whole thing? The tale follows the course of the two policemen assigned to the case. It takes them across several counties as they try to get to the bottom of the missing limb, or was it a complete body?

<u>Revised Edition</u>

This trilogy, No Trace, No Panic and No Fear, was written before the Coronavirus pandemic struck in 2020. Social distancing and the wearing of masks were not an issue.

x

The trilogy are best read in order

No Trace

No Panic

No Fear

Chapter One

The shed door thudded quietly shut behind her and Emilia swore under her breath, 'Damn, can't see'. Emilia knew the layout of her shed like the back of her hand and had no fear of walking across the flag stones to the bench on the other side in order to pick up the three flower pots that she had placed there earlier.

In the darkness, she stumbled and swore again. 'For goodness' sake, Emilia, get a grip', she said to herself. She knelt down to feel what the obstruction was, for it had not been there 20 minutes before. She had been in the shed sorting through suitable pots for her winter hyacinths, and it had been daylight then. She had been called away by the telephone ringing, and now those few minutes later had meant that in the gathering dusk it was now pitch black in her shed, which had no electric light or window. To her horror, she felt a warm, trousered leg. She screamed without thinking and stumbled backwards, stunned by what she felt.

There was a groan, and Emilia screamed again. Then there was a deathly silence. After a few seconds, Emilia pushed herself backwards towards the door on her bottom. Reaching the door, she managed to open it and with a final push, she was outside in the cold night air. After a few seconds, she had gathered her senses enough to know that she had to make an emergency call. No, she had not imagined that warm trousered leg; why else would she have stumbled? Slowly she came to the conclusion that she did in fact have a body in her shed, and then the questions flooded into her mind. Was it male or female, was the person alive or could they be dead or badly injured? Why had it groaned and then gone completely silent? How had that person got into her shed? She had not seen anyone pass her kitchen window, where she had been standing during the telephone call of only a few minutes before. How could so much have happened in a few brief minutes?

Feeling nauseous and shaky on her feet, Emilia struggled up and made herself walk to the back door and the welcome light of the kitchen. Despite the falling rain, she paused momentarily at the door, fearing for a brief moment that there might be someone in the house. After all, she had just discovered a body, alive or dead in her shed, and there was no rhyme or reason for it to be there or indeed for any of this to be happening. Willing herself on, she forced herself to go inside. She was pleased for the warmth and familiarity of her home. Her mind was racing again now. How could this be happening? All she had wanted was those flower pots. She could have left going back for them till morning. Everything is better in the daylight. Then perhaps none of this would be happening. Was that irrational? Maybe there would be a perfectly good explanation for that trousered leg.

'Really? Come on, Emilia, get a grip,' she told herself again. Reaching for the telephone, she carefully selected the three nines. Her mind was racing, and even though the call was answered directly and in the usual calm and efficient manner, all kinds of doubts had flooded through her mind in the meantime. Was this real, had she imagined the last five minutes? For that was all it had taken for these major events to have taken place. Less than it would take for her to peel a pan full of potatoes. But that warm leg had been real.

She was brought back to the present by a cool and efficient voice saying, 'Emergency operator, which service do you require?'

After a moment's hesitation, 'I am rather difficult to find,' Emilia gasped.

'That will not be a problem,' the operator replied, 'and which service?' The tone continued coolly and efficiently, and with a hint of urgency.

'Police and ambulance, I think, there isn't a fire, so just those two please.' Even as she said it, she knew she was rambling, and realised that she had to pull herself together. She had been a university lecturer, she must be able to cope in a crisis.

'And the postcode and house name or number?' the efficient operator continued.

Emilia gave the postcode and house name, 'Gulls Retreat', and continued with directions. 'Take the second left as you come into the hamlet and then turn in down the track by the old pub. There is only me at the end; I'll put all the lights on, please ask them to be as quick as possible, I have a body in my shed.'

Emilia's voice trailed off. Did I really just say that? she thought. She remembered the feel of the warm trousered leg and re-heard the groan. No, she was not dreaming, it really had happened.

Daisy had been an emergency operator for long enough to tell a genuine call. There was always something in the voice, some little extra edge, which could not be fabricated in a hoax call. Daisy had had many of those, and with the countless courses that she had been on, she was now well-respected among her colleagues and peers to be one of the most capable and competent on her team. Daisy continued, 'I have connected with the relevant services, would you like to stay on the line until they reach you?'

'Yes please.' Emilia was grateful for that last comforting suggestion. Here she was down a farm track, at the entrance to which was a derelict pub. All there was nearby was a group of old farm cottages, most of which were holiday or second homes. At this time of year, the Sunday at the end of the October half-term week, they were all locked up and would be now until Christmas.

The emergency services' personnel started talking to Emilia. It was indeed a comfort, and helped to pass what seemed like hours, though it was in fact forty minutes. They were taking her seriously; the police and an ambulance crew raced towards the sleepy hamlet of Beeny.

Chapter Two

Detective Chief Inspector Gavin Freeman and Detective Constable Ore Soloman climbed out of their cars outside Emilia's house. It had now started to rain again, a consistent and persistent stream, quite usual for this part of Cornwall on the North coast. At least it had eased off from the torrential downpour of a few hours earlier. The house which they now approached was well-illuminated, with lights shining in all the windows, and they did not have to wait long on the doorstep. They were greeted by Emilia, who was looking pale and ashen.

'Emilia Sedgewick?'

'Yes,' came the shaky reply.

'I am DCI Freeman and this is DC Soloman, may we come in?'

Emilia seemed to momentarily hesitate as if afraid to let the police officers in, but it was more an uncertainty connected with the evening's events.

Standing in the tiled hall, Freeman spoke, 'You have called us, because you say you have a body in your shed.' Emilia wasn't sure if this was a statement or a question.

'Yes' she replied, 'I went to the shed to collect some garden pots about an hour ago, and in the darkness, I stumbled on something. I bent down and felt a trousered leg. After the initial shock, I managed to get back into the house. I'd only been in the shed in the daylight twenty minutes before that.' Emilia seemed more composed and articulate now.

'You had better show us this shed. Soloman, fetch the torches from the car.'

Two minutes later, Emilia was leading the way down the path to the shed. The outside light had been switched on, and the path glistened in the rain which was still falling. Soloman pulled up the collar of his three-quarter length raincoat. He was a tall and attractive man, of Caribbean descent, new to the area, and dressed in smart dark blue jeans and a black long-sleeved T-shirt. He had a kind, wide smile showing a perfect set of white teeth.

On reaching the shed, Emilia stepped to one side, 'It's in there,' she whispered fearfully, pointing inside.

Freeman pushed open the door and shone his torch around the darkness. Soloman caught up and went inside also shining his torch. The interior of the shed was neat and tidy; over on the far side was the bench that Emilia had already described, and yes, there were the three flower pots, ready for collection. On the left, there were garden tools

7

neatly arranged against the wall, while on the right, bunches of herbs and flowers were hanging to dry from nails in the rafters. The stone-built shed with its slate floor, seemed neat and organised and apart from a rake that was lying on the floor, nothing seemed out of place.

'You say that you felt a trousered leg?' Freeman asked. There was a hint of disbelief in his voice.

'What do you mean?' Emilia asked. She had not yet looked inside, terrified of what she might see.

'There's nobody here,' Soloman added in a matter-of-fact manner, before Freeman could say anything further. 'Only a spillage on the floor, quite a large one by the looks of things, over here.'

'Are you quite sure?' Emilia's voice quavered.

'Absolutely and completely sure.' Freeman responded with clarity.

After a moment, Emilia followed Freeman inside to where Soloman was standing over a glistening pool of dark liquid.

'But there was definitely something in here. I tripped over it.' Fear and trepidation had crept back into Emilia's voice. 'I don't understand,' she faltered.

'And you say you have seen no one all evening, no one prowling around?' Freeman continued. 'It all seems very odd, did this leg have any weight to it, as if it was attached to a body?'

'Yes, that's why I said I had a body in my shed. I never saw anything, but the weight made me believe that there was a body attached to the leg.'

Emilia began to look worried. Had she dreamt the whole escapade, had a funny turn, banged her head, or had there really been a body in her shed not more than an hour ago that had now disappeared? Freeman saw the worried look on Emilia's face. She was beginning to tremble visibly and looked as if she might faint at any moment.

Impulsively he turned to Soloman, 'Call forensics, I know it is late on a Sunday, but they need to investigate this. You wait here for them, while I take Emilia back inside. Take my arm,' Freeman said, turning to Emilia and softening his voice, 'I can't have you falling again this evening.'

Once back in the warmth and security of the house, Emilia felt a little better. The ambulance crew who had arrived at the same time as Freeman and Soloman and who were all prepared for looking at a body, were feeling redundant. They had dutifully followed the police inspectors through the house to the shed. As there was no body, they looked confused and as such sat Emilia down and asked her if she was alright, seeing that she was shaken by her experience. They did their usual checks and finding her none the worse, they left Gulls Retreat.

Clearly something was afoot; firstly there had been a body on the floor of the shed, secondly it had then disappeared seemingly without a trace, and this had all happened in the quietest of locations when there was nobody about. Emilia looked at DCI Freeman and was relieved that he now looked pensive. At least it looks as though he believes me and is taking this seriously. Her chain of thought was broken by the DCI speaking, 'I think, in the circumstances, I had better organise some door-to-door enquiries starting tomorrow.'

Emilia wasn't quite sure what this had to do with her, perhaps he was just thinking out loud, she thought.

'Do you have anyone who can be with you tonight?' He carried on hurriedly. There was a moment's pause while she contemplated this question.

'No, not really,' she replied. 'Although I have lived here many years, I am a very private person and I don't know anyone well enough.'

'That's alright,' he continued, 'I'll arrange for a family liaison officer to spend the night here. Do you mind if I have a quick look round, upstairs? It helps with the investigation if we have checked all aspects.'

'Be my guest,' Emilia said, 'it's all tidy up there.' She was tired and confused by the evening's events. Her ordered, calm and peaceful existence had been shattered. She was too upset to mind letting a strange man up to the more private areas of her home, even if he was a policeman. But she did not appreciate the real reason why Freeman wanted to look upstairs. To Freeman, everyone was a suspect until proven otherwise and he knew that although it was unlikely that Emilia had anything further here to do with the case, he would have to prove that he had checked Gulls Retreat.

He quickly went upstairs. The stairway was wide and opened onto a spacious landing. The old polished oak floorboards creaked gently under his footsteps. There was a large window to the front which in daylight hours would light the landing and stairway. The plainly painted walls had two spectacular wave paintings, presumably created by a local artist. Once upstairs, Freeman saw four open doors. Three led to bedrooms and one to a bathroom. Freeman respectfully moved between the rooms. All were plainly decorated, with newly refurbished old oak floorboards and tasteful rugs. White wooden shutters enclosed the windows and coastal scene artwork decorated the walls. White bed linen complemented the oak bed frames. The rooms were simply furnished but as Freeman looked around he appreciated that there was no shortage of money here.

The oak boards continued to creak here and there. The first two bedrooms were set out as guest rooms and the third, the main bedroom, was tidy, but obviously used by Emilia. The bathroom had recently been refurbished to a high standard in white. There was nothing to suggest that anything was amiss. The rooms were clean and tidy and there were no smells of bleach or cleaning products.

Freeman took photos of the rooms and landing. If any future evidence suggested otherwise, then forensics would have to look more deeply into Gulls Retreat. At the moment we are looking at a missing body discovered in an outside shed, and there is nothing to suggest that the body was ever inside, thought Freeman. I don't want to upset this old lady anymore than she already is.

He retraced his steps back downstairs, where he found Emilia looking pale and exhausted on the sofa.

'I'll just take some photos down here, for our records,' Freeman announced. There wasn't an option. Downstairs was open plan, wrapping around the central hall and staircase. A kitchen at the front on one side led to a dining area, lounge, and then to more of a study or snug on the opposite side of the house to the kitchen. All was presented in a homely manner, clean and tidy. This is no crime scene, thought Freeman.

'Thank you for letting me look around. You have a lovely home.' Freeman sounded more like a prospective purchaser than a policeman, and that perhaps was intentional. 'Fiona Fielding will be along shortly, to keep you company this evening. She's very understanding.'

With that, he picked up his coat and left.

DC Soloman was just coming through the back door as the DCI was leaving at the front.

'Forensics have just arrived,' he said, 'so I'll be off then.' He paused briefly aware that he should check first before leaving, 'Is there anything else I can do?'

'The other detective said that he would organise for someone to be with me tonight. Do you think that you might be able to stay until she arrives? I am feeling rather lost.' Then as if to add some bargaining into the request, she added, 'I have some stew here, freshly made in the slow cooker. I am sure you could do with some supper.'

It was now seven thirty and the detective constable was beginning to feel hungry, so he agreed to stay and keep Emilia company.

A little while later, after Soloman had finished his second plate of stew, the doorbell rang and when he opened the door, he was greeted by the family liaison officer. Checking once again that Emilia was happy to be left, he departed, promising to return in the morning.

PC Fiona Fielding was a competent and professional police constable with several years of experience. She was good at her job, well liked within her team with a wicked sense of humour and a naughty smile. On occasions such as these she had a calm and reassuring manner. She was also good at lightening the mood. As she walked into the living room, where Emilia was sat, she breezily introduced herself and continued on with, 'I am sorry I have been so long: I popped into the late night store to collect rations.' She proudly held up a carrier bag in which could be seen several packets of biscuits and various chocolate bars. 'At times like these I hate to come empty handed. Tea, we always seem to drink so much tea and I do like something to dunk. Now let me check on forensics, then I'll lock up and put the kettle on. You can tell me all about it over a cuppa.'

Emilia liked this orderliness and immediately felt she could trust this young woman, who was young enough to be her granddaughter.

An hour and a half later, forensics were just finishing, 'we have checked for fingerprints, footprints and anything else that there might be a trace of, and of course taken a sample of that liquid on the floor. You will find crime scene tape surrounding the area,' the more senior of the two said. He was a tall, grey haired man competent in his job and used to being called out at odd hours. 'The whole area must not be disturbed, but it is too late to do anything further this evening.' With that, he and his colleague left.

There was a pause, while Emilia gathered herself. She looked at Fiona, 'what do you think that liquid is on the floor?'

Fiona knew that she could not commit herself. That was not part of her job this evening. She smiled, 'I am sure we will find out in due course.'

Emilia felt weary all of a sudden and rising to her feet, she said, 'I think my bed calls'.

Chapter Three

Professor Emilia Sedgewick was an energetic seventy two year old, who had lived in the small hamlet of Beeny, near Boscastle, for twelve years. She was short in stature at five foot two and of petit build. She had moved to the hamlet with her husband, Bertie, also a professor but sadly he had passed away two years before. They had moved from Oxford, where they had been the backbone of the university. Well known in their respective fields, they had decided that enough was enough and after a full on academic and social life in the city, they now needed to slow down and enjoy their retirement together.

The decision to move had not been hard especially when they found the house in Beeny. After extensive renovations, they had quickly settled into their new home and life. They had decided to keep their lives quiet and although they were well known in the area, no one knew too much about them. Having dedicated their lived to medicine, there had been no time for children and as a result, having lost her dearest husband, there was no one else, apart from her elder brother. He had never left the family home town of Lewes in Sussex. Although he had always been very close to Emilia, their lives had naturally grown apart and coupled with the distance between Sussex and Cornwall, they had only seen each other a few times a year.

Emilia was slow to move the following morning. Understandably she had not slept well and as the early morning light crept upon Beeny, she was dozing quietly on her bed. A cold cup of tea sat on the bedside table next to her, with the remains of a chocolate digestive biscuit in the saucer. PC Fielding had brought it to her after she had retired upstairs, but she had fallen asleep soon after, only to waken three hours later. She had been restless since that time, the events of the previous evening casting dark shadows in her mind. In the darkness of the night she had tried to recollect the order and timings of what had happened. Try as she might, none of it made any sense.

She was woken by a knock on the bedroom door. Emilia opened her eyes and before she could speak, a smiling face appeared, 'Good morning, I've brought you a cup of tea. How did you sleep?'

PC Fielding exchanged the cups of tea on the cabinet and stood back.

'Good morning, I've slept for a few hours here and there, thank you.' Emilia managed a weak smile.

'There is no need to rush this morning. DCI Freeman will be along later. He has messaged me this morning to see how you are.'

'How was your night?' Emilia said as she roused herself and sat up. 'Where you alight downstairs? You know that you could have had the spare bedroom up here.'

'I was fine, thank you. I am quite used to sleeping in a chair.'

Fielding did not wish to stress the point that she was on duty and thankfully there had been no further incidents in the night that she was aware of. All had been quiet.... but then all had been quiet during that eventful hour the night before.

PC Fielding returned downstairs and busied herself tidying the kitchen.

Half an hour later, there was a knock on the door and Freeman and Soloman were standing on the front step. Fielding took them through to the large open plan living room at the rear of the house. Freeman strode to the window where he gazed out at the garden. Soloman could see that he was deep in thought.

'I'll make teas and coffees when Emilia comes down,' Fielding cheerfully reported. 'I'll just announce you.'

Freeman and Soloman exchanged glances, once a

thespian, always a thespian,' Freeman said under his breath as Fielding exited into the hallway. 'We should have another look around this room while we wait.'

'What for?' Soloman answered slightly bewildered.

'Anything and everything, this house does not appear to be a crime scene, but we can't rule it out, especially in these early days. Look at the room with fresh eyes and see if anything looks out of place or unusual.'

Soloman responded with a thumbs up sign and began looking.

Ten minutes later, Emilia appeared in an expensive pink silk dressing gown. It was very apparent that she had just risen from her bed. As she entered, Freeman and Soloman turned from where they had been looking around the room.

'You have a fantastic view and such a large garden. This is a wonderful spot.' Freeman started, 'I had no idea but it was dark last night. I am sorry to be here again. Soloman and I need to ask you a few more questions and run over again what happened last evening.'

Emilia settled herself down. She was used to her visitors complimenting her on the view and her garden. After more questions and a repetition of what had happened last night, the DCI finished by saying, 'We do have house to house enquiries starting this morning. Someone must have seen somebody or at least heard a car. We should get some forensic results back before the end of the day. Can you think of anything else, anything occurred to you in the night?'

'I've been over it all a dozen times. I'm sorry, I can't think of anything further at the moment.'

Freeman paused and then with a smile he continued, 'we will check over the garden and driveway and have another look around by the shed. We may have missed something in the dark.'

As the two of them disappeared out of the French doors, Emilia noticed that a sea mist was beginning to descend. She was quite used to this phenomena. Now it added a further gloom and despondency to the day.

Freeman and Soloman walked over to the vegetable plot at the far end of the garden and started to meticulously search the area. It was a dismal job in the descending mist poking around in the remnants of Emilia's vegetables. Wetness clung to the remains of the plants and both of them found that their shoes had quickly clogged with soil. Soon after, they were clear and walking down the far boundary by the wall, along the edge of the lawn. Progress was slow, not helped by the weather, but the two policemen were used to this repetitive work and carried on unperturbed. However their searching was in vain and they found no clues. A further look down the back and front of the shed did not produce any evidence either. Eventually they made their way to the front of the house, but sadly after searching the parking area and garage, they still had no more clues or evidence to work on.

In the track between the cottages, that ran along the rear of Emilia's garden, two police constables had arrived and started knocking on the doors. There was no answer at numbers one, two or three. It appeared that they were all locked up but despite this there was definite evidence that the cottages had been occupied recently. Steps and paths had been swept. Windows were clean and free of cobwebs, bushes and shrubs had been cut back and curtains and blinds had been drawn and lowered.

However number four was different. The front door had little paint on it. The little that was present, was flaky and very old, the colour indeterminate though years of sunlight and wear. The windows were filthy, dusty on the outside and thick with grease on the inside. The torn net curtain was stuck to the glass. Nothing of the interior could be seen, such was the dirt. A feeble fifteen watt light bulb glowed dimly.

Having knocked on the door and after what seemed like an eternity, there was the sound of shuffling from within. It was eventually opened revealing an elderly gentleman, scruffy in appearance and unkempt. He appeared to have one leg shorter than the other and as he moved back from the door he limped. The trouser leg on that side was rolled up. A dirty and blood soaked bandage was wrapped around the exposed limb. His face was pale and grey and his eyes were deeply sunk into the lined and wrinkled face. The was no sparkle in those eyes. A long grey beard added nothing positive to his appearance.

The smell of stale urine wafted past him and out into the open air. Opening the door also partly revealed the interior which followed suit. It was dirty and there was rubbish piled high, making access difficult. The extent of the smell, detritus and general demeanour of the gentleman standing in front of them took the two policemen aback, and although both of them had been trained in the unexpected, this was a step a little greater than even they were used to.

Pulling himself together and holding up his identification, the first constable spoke, 'Good morning sir, we are sorry to disturb you. We are police constables making house to house enquiries and wondered if you had heard anything unusual last evening, any extra cars or people that you had not seen before?'

The man looked momentarily taken aback. His world had been interrupted and he wasn't used to this. He gazed at the pair as if he had been removed from his world and placed into another. He continued to lift his eyes from one to the other. His eyes were lifeless and the whites had a yellowish tinge.

The two policemen looked at each other. They had been taught that in circumstances such as these, patience was the best option. Eventually and with great effort, he answered, 'I haven't seen anything.' He shuffled slightly as if he was making to return indoors.

'Are you quite sure?' the first policeman asked.

'I just told you, didn't I?' There was a note of aggression in his voice.

The second policeman was staring at the man's bandaged leg, 'What happened there?' he asked pointing at the leg.

There was a moments pause, and the man seemed confused.

'None of your business,' came the answer as the door was pushed firmly shut. The noise was solid and final.

'I should get that leg looked at, looks nasty,' the second policeman just managed to say before there was the sound of heavy bolts being drawn across the door.

The policemen exchanged glances again. 'We will make a note of this property. That leg looks interesting. We will come back with a search warrant if we need to. That is the only way we will get in, I think.'

Cottages five and six were as closed as the first three. Number five had a key safe screwed to the wall and a holiday cottage accreditation sticker in the window.

Freeman and Soloman stood at the end of the lane as they waited for the policemen to finish. 'Let me have your findings as soon as possible,' Freeman barked.

He and Soloman turned around and returned to Emilia's garden. They walked back up and entered the house from the south facing terrace. Soloman had a brief image of lazy days sunbathing there with a cooling drink in hand. It was dispelled by the sound of Freeman's voice, 'Those cottages with their gardens that all back onto yours, do you know much about the owners? The house to house team are not getting much response from their knocking.

22

The six terraced cottages, that Freeman was referring to, were the original farm workers dwellings. Their gardens were one hundred foot in length and twelve foot wide. On the other side of them was a track that provided access to their front doors. There was another row on the other side of this track.

'I'm afraid I don't really know much about the owners,' Emilia replied, 'I know that one of them, number four, is lived in by a recluse. No one sees him, just occasionally he is seen shuffling to the bus stop. As for the others, I believe that they are either second homes or rented out for holiday use through agencies. I always make a point of being friendly, waving and saying good morning. Some people I recognize from holiday period to holiday period but I am never sure if they are owners or repeat holidaymakers. I have seen children come and grow up over the twelve odd years that I have been here. I hope that helps.'

'It does and it doesn't,' Freeman said rather too abruptly. 'It means that we will have to question further afield which all adds to the workload.' He sighed wearily.

He's being a bit unfair. Soloman thought. Emilia was only answering his question.

This was not the first time that Freeman had dealt with the possibility of a dead body. But a missing body, with no one living in the locality, a row of empty properties, and no evidence in the house or garden, all created more work. Resources were already stretched to their limit and he was only now coming to terms with sharing his team with the

Devon force. Theirs was a much bigger and diverse county and they weren't always overly helpful with sharing with their poorer neighbours. On reflection he realized that the empty cottages would provide many places to hide a potential body. He sighed again. In the silence it was noticeable, but he saw his workload increasing significantly and all because a seventy two year old thought that she had felt a body part in the dark.

Freeman broke the silence that they had fallen into, 'We had another look at the shed and around the back of it. It all seems secure with no obvious way someone could have got in round the boundary. You have stone walls with plants growing amongst the ragged rocks on the tops and none seem to show signs of someone climbing over, let alone dragging a body. What you reported,' he said addressing Emilia directly, 'was that you thought that the trouser material was denim.'

'Yes, that is correct.'

'Are you sure that there is nothing else?' There was desperation in his tone now. It was day two and there was no progress.

Emilia's reply was not what he was expecting, 'Do you need me after tomorrow? I am going to ring my brother in Lewis and see if I can visit him for a week. I am feeling stronger now and I can manage tonight on my own. I would prefer to have a night alone before I go, then I know that I will be able to manage when I return. I don't lock the shed, so you can get in and out as you wish.'

'I don't think that will be a problem but we will need

to speak with you after we have the forensics report back. That will be tomorrow. After that you can visit your brother. Give your mobile number and brother's landline to DC Soloman.'

'Thank you, I could do with a break.'

Within five minutes the two police constables and Freeman and Soloman had left and Emilia breathed a sigh, grateful to have the house to herself. She sat down and telephoned her brother, Robert. It was now mid-afternoon and despite a strong determination on her part not to become emotional, her brother soon detected a quivering in her voice. They had always been close. As a result, it had not been hard to detect. Reluctantly she had had to explain what had happened. She would have preferred to do this on arrival as she felt it would make more sense in person.

Robert, who was a kind and caring brother, listened intently but found that Emilia's recollections of the past hours did not make much sense. In the end, after tears had come and gone, he decided to wait for another version when she arrived. Despite the lengthy journey he even considered driving to Cornwall to collect her. However, she managed to persuade him that she could manage to drive the distance.

Emilia put the phone down and sat for a moment. At least that hurdle was over and she could refocus in Lewis and be looked after by her brother and sister in law.

She made her way upstairs and ran a bath. After a relaxing soak, during which she could not make any sense of the last twenty four hours, she packed a small suitcase, made a light supper and prepared for an early night. She retired to bed with a book and some light music.

Chapter Four

DCI Gavin Freeman was thirty five and married with a young daughter. As he sat in his kitchen on the new estate in Bodmin feeding her the following morning, he was completely perplexed. He simply could not make head nor tail of the facts as they presented themselves. He went over it all again. The house to house team had revealed nothing, no body had been discovered, nobody had been reported missing, and apart from a pool of blood in a shed, there seemed to be nothing untoward, only the report from a seventy-two year old woman who said she had felt a trousered human leg in the dark, in her all-too-familiar shed which she had left unoccupied only twenty minutes before.

He set off for work, leaving his wife to take their

young daughter to nursery. He felt that it was going to be another long day. Twenty minutes later, sitting at his desk in the police station, Freeman was reading the forensic report that had been emailed though. The report revealed that it was indeed female human blood that had been found in the shed. That was a step forward, but still there was that nagging series of doubts. If there had been a body, why had it been there for such a short period of time? They only had Emilia's word and she might have had a temporary lapse or become confused. But Freeman discounted these random thoughts as quickly as they had entered his mind. Perhaps someone had moved it, or had the person regained consciousness, got up and walked out? Again the latter seemed a little far-fetched, and he put it to one side. So if the body was moved, who had moved it, and where was it now? Visions of grisliness came into his mind as he pondered these thoughts.

Three hundred miles away in Manchester, Matthew Ford was deliberating with his mobile phone whether to telephone the police. It was now Tuesday morning and an hour before, he had received a call from the surgery, where his estranged wife was a GP, to say that for the second day running, she had failed to arrive for work. He had been asked if he had any idea where she might be. There had been no answer on her mobile and one of the surgery team who lived nearby had knocked on her door, on the way to work that morning. Again there had been no response.

He and his wife did not see much of each other now. She had remained in Bristol after they had split up. Matthew had moved and joined a prestigious firm of accountants in Manchester. Both were doing very well in their respective careers. Their two sons aged nine and eleven were at a private boarding school.

Matthew made a decision and dialed one zero one, the non-emergency police number. His details were taken and a file made on the national database for a possible missing person. Matthew was asked to provide further details, a recent photo of his wife and if possible, an idea of her recent movements. They seemed to be taking him seriously although there was a suggestion that as his wife was an adult and it had only been two days and they were now leading separate lives, perhaps it was a bit early to be filing a missing person report. Matthew agreed but when he further explained that he had just spent the last week with his estranged wife and two sons on half-term in a friend's holiday home in north Cornwall, the police civilian agreed that there might be more to this. He appreciated that if the woman in question was missing, the husband might have been one of the last to see her.

Half an hour later, an alert popped up on Freeman's computer screen. Whenever a missing person report was filed, he received a warning email. Freeman did what he usually did when this happened, a casual glance, a quick read, then back to what he was concentrating on. But something made him sit up, 'half term, missing female, North Cornwall'. Freeman sat and thought for a few minutes. Could there be a connection between this missing person and his current case? He realised that this was a possible break-through. Now he had a missing person, maybe she was from his area. Freeman picked up his jacket and collected Soloman from his desk, sprinting down the stairs and out to his car.

'What's up, boss, why the urgency?' Soloman panted behind him.

'Missing person alert from Bristol, possibly gone missing from our area, maybe part of our Beeny case,' Freeman stated, as he put his car into gear and accelerated out of the police headquarters.

'We must check the area around Gulls Retreat again ourselves, more thoroughly. I am convinced we have missed a major part of this case. We need to review everything again, look at everything from every angle. We must have missed a vital clue.'

There was an increasing use of the word 'every' and Freeman became more and more animated. His driving became erratic, his hands moved off the steering wheel with exaggerated flourishes and his head turned left and right quickly at the road junctions. Soloman had seen Freeman like this before and had learnt to remain silent and listen. Freeman was generally a docile and relaxed boss, but then in certain situations his mood could change.

On this particular morning, the sun was shining brightly as they made their way across country towards the coast. The leaves on the trees were turning to the lovely autumnal golds, yellows and browns. The roads were dry and the air was warm. It was almost like a positive omen. This was unlike the last few days which had alternated between a thick sea mist and rain.

The extra traffic created by half term had

dissipated and the roads were less congested. The wind turbines along the top were gradually turning and it seemed that all was well with the world.

Soloman kept quiet and let Freeman fill him in on all the details.

'And another thing,' he said, getting more animated again as he realised he had just thought of something further to investigate, 'get hold of this Matthew Ford now and find out where they have been staying down here in Cornwall. We will have to check it out whether it be a hotel, bed and breakfast, second home or holiday let.'

Soloman made mental notes. Forty minutes later, they coasted into Beeny and came to a halt outside the derelict pub at the end of the track that led to Gulls Retreat. It was now just before noon on Tuesday and Beeny was basking in warm sunshine. The wind had dropped and if it had been a touch warmer, it would have seemed like a summer's day. The heavy dew had all but disappeared. Silence reigned, the shadows were longer and the yet-to-fall leaves had deepened in colour. Even the screeching gulls that usually swooped high and low overhead seemed to be having a rest and were nowhere to be seen.

Freeman set off at a pace down the track with Soloman hard on his heels, determined to give the place a thorough going-over again. As they neared the house, they could see Emilia's parked car with the boot open. She was preparing to leave for Lewis. The front door was open, but the rest of Gulls Retreat appeared to be locked up with shutters across the windows. As they reached the porch, Emilia approached with a small case.

'I rather presumed that you would be back today,' Emilia offered. 'Any news back regarding the forensics, I am anxious to get off to Lewis?'

'Yes the initial reports are back, and I am happy that we have no more questions for you at present. We shall be investigating further here today, but outside, so you are free to set off for Lewis when you are ready. Any idea how long you are likely to be away?'

'About a week, I think.'

Freeman nodded implying that Emilia was free to leave. She climbed into the car and drove off down the track. Freeman had decided that he would test Emilia's mental capacity through conversation, when she returned. Having given her a break and rest from what had obviously been a terrible shock, he would be able to see if she told the same story.

'It's strange that she didn't ask about the forensic results,' Freeman said, 'but I suppose some people don't think and perhaps she just wanted to get away as quickly as possible.'

He looked up at the house. It was attractive with its large and well-proportioned windows set within the solid granite walls. The large glass porch with its wide and gracious steps gave the property a friendly and welcoming appearance.

'It's not the house that I am bothered with. I don't believe that there is anything suspicious inside having looked extensively on the first evening. No, any crime committed here, was outside.' Freeman explained. 'I want to have another look around the back of the shed and down that track where the cottages are. Start here with me,' he barked as they rounded the corner of the shed and looked behind it.

A flagstone path encircled it, and next to that was a boundary stone wall. Beyond this was a field, on a level with the top of the stone wall. There was therefore a drop into Emilia's garden. It was a grazing field but was empty of stock now.

Half way down this wall, there was something that made Soloman stop. Some of the stones in the wall were jutting out, creating an easy step up the wall to the field above. A post and rail fence was positioned about a metre within the boundary to prevent any grazing stock from falling into Emilia's garden. Soloman took a photo on his iPhone and would have summoned Freeman, but he had disappeared from view and was further down the garden examining another wall along the southern boundary.

Soloman climbed up the makeshift rungs onto the field at the top. Turning left, he walked along the edge of the field next to the post and rail fence. He soon reached the corner of the field and found a gate through onto the track. It showed signs of occasional use. The brambles that had tried to grow across the path were dried and brittle from walkers pushing past and trampling over them. It led down to the track between the cottages.

Soloman vaulted over the gate, his athletic frame coming to the fore. There was a large clearing on the right hand side before the end cottage, number six. This rough piece of land was used for parking and turning. Once it had been graveled but now it was rutted and full of weeds.

Around the edges there were bushes and trees, which had not been cleared for many years. They would make a wonderful place for children to play. The trees were big enough to climb and the undergrowth was dense enough to make dens. Soloman thought back to his own childhood. He could just remember as a very small lad, how exciting these places were, before electronic devices and phones had taken the place of these innocent past times. It would be unclear who owned this patch of ground as was often the case in country areas.

It was still sunny, but a stiff sea breeze was getting up. Soloman was beginning to feel more enthused now. He and Freeman had come out to have another attempt at finding out what had happened here, and as he started out down the track, his eye was caught by something on his right. Just before the first cottage, at this end, number 6, he saw something black at just below knee height, sticking out of the undergrowth.

Soloman strode over and pulled apart the shrubbery. To his amazement he found himself staring at the back of a dark-coloured car. Pulling the bushes further apart he walked around it slowly. The front bumper was badly dented and scratched and the back window wiper was hanging off. Soloman stood there for a minute, absorbing what was in front of him. Having taken stock, he turned around, raced to the gate which he again vaulted over and retraced his steps back into the garden.

He found Freeman absorbed in a phone call. He

finished quickly when he saw Soloman's face and gesticulations suggesting that he should follow him. Freeman was surprised at the route he was being taken and even more surprised when Soloman pulled aside the bushes to reveal the dark car. After a moment's pause, Freeman said, 'This looks interesting, better get the full handle on what is going on here. Do a PNC check on that plate, can you?'

'Already in progress, boss.' Between the pair of them, they did a full investigation of the car. They managed to reach the driver's door which surprisingly opened very easily. There were sweets and crisp wrappers in the footwells and on the back seat there were empty Coke and energy drink bottles. When they lifted the boot lid, they found a suitcase.

'Any sign of a mobile, or a handbag?' Freeman asked. 'Better search the immediate area also.'

Their extensive search of the car and nearby undergrowth drew a blank.

'Better come back another day and look further afield for these missing items.' Freeman said. 'In the meantime we had better get forensics on this so organise a truck to take it back to the yard. That suitcase should tell us a great deal, and all of a sudden we seem to have turned a corner. I knew if we had another search we should find something, so excellent work Soloman, not like the door-to-door enquiries which have missed all of this.'

The truck was ordered, and an hour later, it had been loaded and was on its way to the police yard. At that moment Soloman's phone rang and a well spoken voice at the other end announced that he was Matthew Ford returning Soloman's call.

'What can you tell us about where you were staying on your recent trip to Cornwall?'

'We were staying in a holiday cottage belonging to close friends of my estranged wife, Lorretta. We've stayed in it many times over the years. It's almost like a second home to us. Although it holds many happy memories of when we were together, it still remains a good place for us to go, and the boys love it.'

'Your sons?' Soloman wanted the last point clarified.

'Yes, Peter and Luke.'

'And how old are they?'

'Eleven and nine.'

'And the address of this holiday cottage?'

Matthew gave the address and stated that it would now be empty. He believed that their friends, the owners, would be staying there next at Christmas.

'And what are their names and their permanent address,' Soloman asked.

'Debbie and Andrew Garrod,' Matthew replied. He gave a Bath address.

After further checks had been made, the results on the car came back as being fully insured with a current MOT and registered to a Lorretta Ford of

Clifton,Bristol.

Chapter Five

'I think that we had better get off to Bristol,' Freeman said forty-five minutes later when they were back at headquarters in Bodmin.

Ore Soloman was used to having his free evenings dissipate in front of him. Very often, detective work required a change of plan at the last minute. As I am new here, he thought, and this looks like an interesting case, I had better prove myself. It might be the break I am looking for.

He had arrived from his home town of Reading four months before. His learning curve had been intense and there had been no time to make any new friends. Although he believed that policing in the South West was going to be more mundane,

Soloman understood that there would be more chance for him to excel.

The first few months had followed a routine. Being the summer holidays, policing had been a different ball game. As he had settled into his new job and life, he had been spared the more gritty aspects of detective work common to the needs of a heavily populated and busy town like Reading. He had spent most of his time with the traffic division, coming to terms with the comparative isolation of the Cornish towns and villages. He now understood the main roads, even they were smaller, the tiny lanes and the complete absence of motorways.

He had filled a vacancy in the force created by Bill who had retired. They were two completely different characters. Bill was old school, and some would say that it was past his time for retirement. He had always been in the police force. As a child he had grown up with one desire, to serve his local community. But now, fifty years later, policing was completely different. He found that he simply did not understand the new methods. He had become stubborn and vocal to his superiors when change was implemented. Bill was Cornish and as such understood the ways of the local people, but now as more people had moved into the county, the needs of the populous were gradually changing. The interview board had decided that someone young and from a different area, preferably a city or large town conurbation, would be the ideal and preferred candidate to fit the vacancy.

Ore Soloman had arrived, with fresh ideas, and although he had found the Cornish friendly and welcoming, there had been a tendency for slight suspicion, but only because he was an unknown quantity. In the first few months, he had settled into his new role, shown his work colleagues that he was a dedicated, hard worker and fun team player. Now with this case, he really had something to engage his mind.

Ore had managed to find a reasonable one bedroom flat to rent. It was on the edge of a new estate in Bodmin, and although he had been given a car, he usually walked the short distance to the Police headquarters. He had furnished it simply; there wasn't room for much more than the basics. He had managed to make it homely and felt settled, much to his mother's relief.

'Is it always this wet?' Soloman asked Freeman as they climbed into Freeman's car.   They were setting off for Bristol to try to find the answers to a growing list of questions.

'Yes,' you're in the south west now, wet and breezy.' Freeman had a tendency to paraphrase when his mind was working overtime. It was also a sign of his being in a good mood.

'Not like the airless Thames Valley then, full of fumes.'

What a difference to the warmth of the day. Now they had the smell of rain on warm tarmac. Soloman had certainly found the Cornish weather very invigorating. He slept better and always felt he had more energy.

It was now dark and with the increasing rain, the journey became more tiring as they sped along the main road towards Exeter and then onwards on the motorway.

'I decided that we should go to Bristol instead of relying on the team up there. It's our investigation, which we have started and we know what we are dealing with. They will be too busy anyhow and we aren't under the same constraints.'

He seemed animated and full of energy despite it being late in the day.

Freeman and Soloman discussed the case again; there was the chance that they might think of another scenario. It was always best to have more options.

The traffic had thinned, but the rain had remained at a constant level. As they reached the outskirts of Bristol, they discussed their strategies when they made their two house calls. First on the agenda was the address where the recovered car had been registered. As they pulled up outside the terraced house in the smart street in the up-market area of Clifton, they began to take in their surroundings, the neat little front gardens and smartly painted front doors.

They knocked on the door of number twenty eight, standing by the immaculately clipped bay trees. They waited and knocked and rung the bell again. There was still no reply, no sound from within. They looked up and down the street. It was deserted. Soloman looked up at the first floor windows. All was dark in the house.

'Better try the neighbours,' Freeman said.

They tried the houses either side; at the first, there

41

was no response but at the other, eventually the door was opened and an attractive man in jogging gear appeared. 'Yes?' Richard Edwards said.

'Good evening, we are very sorry to disturb you, I am DCI Freeman and this is DC Soloman. We just wanted to ask you a few questions about your neighbour, next door. How well do you know her and when did you last see her?'

'Been running, sorry haven't seen her today or for several days.'

'Could we come in for a moment, it's very important.'

'Yes of course,' Richard said, backing down the narrow hall so that the two police men could enter. He led them into a large open plan living area. He continued, 'I don't know Lorretta very well, I work long and irregular hours. I am not here very much. What is all this about, has something happened to her?'

'We are not sure at the moment. We are trying to build a picture of her movements over the last few days. Does anyone else live here?'

'No, no one else, sorry, I don't know anymore.'

'Soloman took a few details and handed him his card and stated that that was all for now, and that they might be back.

'Give me a call if you think of anything.'

Just as they were going through the gate, Richard called out, 'I don't remember seeing her car last week, a black Audi estate.'

'When did you last see it?'

'Lorretta usually seems to park outside, not like me. I seem to have to walk half a mile. It must be the hours that I work,' he paused, 'but now that I think about it, I haven't seen it for about ten days. I think she might have gone away.'

'That's very useful, thank you,' Freeman said. 'We'll be in touch.'

'Onto the mother, I think now.' Freeman said, and then added as if an afterthought, 'just a possibility, our missing body might be this Lorretta. She appears to be missing and we have the possibility of a body.....somewhere.'

This was the first time that this last point had been verbally mentioned.

A mile and a half away, they pulled up outside the house belonging to Lorretta's mother. They had been given the address by her estranged husband, when he had first telephoned. The houses in this road were larger and detached. It was now eight o'clock and the rain had eased slightly. There were climbing roses around the two brick columns, bereft now of flowers and a large covered porch with a beautiful tiled floor.

The house was double-fronted and there was a light on in the left hand window. The front door was opened promptly after the first ring.

The lady who opened the door was in her late fifties, although she could have passed for ten years younger. She had the look and stance of a nineteen thirties film star, tall and with timeless beauty. She wore discreet makeup and a tasteful, full-length cream dressing gown.

'Mrs. Spalding?'

'Yes?' she said in a low and comforting but questioning voice.

'We are very sorry to disturb you at this late hour, my name is DCI Freeman and this is DC Soloman. We are attached to the Cornwall constabulary. We are here to ask you some questions about your daughter, Lorretta. May we come in please?'

'Yes please do,' came a rather hesitant response, 'follow me.' A slightly worried tone had crept into her voice.

They followed her into a large kitchen breakfast room. It was a family room opening onto the garden, modern and expensive. Anabella leant elegantly against the extensive granite work tops. 'Is everything alright?'

It was obvious that at this late hour, everything was not alright, but Anabella's question was borne more out of nervousness.

'We have just called at your daughter's house. There was no reply. We called at the neighbours either side. One neighbour answered and informed us that even though he was busy at work, it was unusual for him not to see Lorretta all week, even if it was just her car.'

'My son in law, Matthew, did telephone this

morning to say that he was thinking of calling you to report that my daughter might be missing. He did not ring back, so although I was naturally very concerned, I am not over duly worried. I expect she just thought she had told the surgery she would not be back until tomorrow.'

'It does appear,' Freeman started, 'that there is a possibility that your daughter may be missing. It seems we have found her car abandoned in Cornwall, so either that was planned, and she has gone off with someone else in their car, or something has indeed happened to her. If the former were the case there would be no reason for her secrecy.'

It was true that Lorretta only lived a mile and a half away and she did usually see her once a week. Like her daughter, she too was very busy, though her hectic schedule was more socially based than Lorretta's. She knew and could confirm that her daughter had been on holiday in Cornwall for the duration of the last week with her two boys, who were on half term vacation from their private school.

She had met up with her estranged husband, who now resided and worked in Manchester. He had left the cottage in Cornwall, that they had rented from friends, who lived in Bath, with his sons, Peter and Luke, first thing on the Sunday morning in order to deliver the boys back to their school which was between Bristol and Manchester. Lorretta would leave later, having tidied up.

That, Anabella said, was what had happened, as far as she knew. Indeed her son-in-law and two grandsons had called in for a late lunch as they had passed Bristol, full of lovely holiday stories. The weather had been warm and dry and the week had been a great success for all. Lunch had been and gone, and the good weather had continued that afternoon. The boys had played in the garden on the swing under the old apple tree, until it was time to leave for school and Manchester beyond. They were all completely unaware of what was happening in Cornwall, where only a few hours before they had all been so happy. After Anabella had finished relating her version, she looked quizzically at the two policemen. Freeman looked at Soloman.

'That all seems to make sense and fit in. This is my card, please call me if you have any questions or think of anything, no matter how trivial. Is there anyone your daughter might have visited or knew in the area? It is rather a long shot, but I am thinking of anyone between here and Cornwall, a large area I know, who could give us a heads up on anyone who might be able to help us further.'

Anabella looked pensive.

'I can't think of anyone at the moment, but I will go through my addresses and give it some thought.'

There was a pause, then she said, 'This all sounds so dreadful and terrifying, all out of the blue, I am so shocked.'

The pensive look evaporated and a pale and terrified look took its place. There was a rustle of expensive French silk as Anabella collapsed very gracefully to the floor. She had fainted. The horrifying news that it looked as if her daughter, her only child, might be missing and furthermore that something may have happened to her had caught up and taken its toll.

Thankfully Anabella came around almost immediately. Soloman helped Anabella to her feet and guided her to one of the two leather easy chairs in the corner of the room next to the French doors which overlooked the garden. The two policemen exchanged glances.

'Is there someone we should call Mrs. Spalding?' Soloman asked. 'You have had a nasty shock.'

'I'll be fine,' Anabella said rather shakily, but rallying at the same time. 'If I think of anything, I'll give you a call.'

With that Freeman and Soloman were off into the night and the accompanying drizzle. As they drove off down the motorway, they pondered the evening's events. Had they actually learnt anything new? All they had confirmed was that Matthew Ford had kept his Sunday lunch appointment with his mother-in-law and his two sons. Mrs. Spalding, it appeared knew nothing of her daughter's current whereabouts.

After half an hour of silence, Freeman announced that in the morning, they would go back to Beeny and spread their search wider as there had to be something as yet undiscovered. In fact, there was a great deal to be discovered, as they had no fresh leads from this trip to Bristol. In theory they had a missing person, perhaps a body, which could now be anywhere. Hopefully Lorretta, was somewhere between Beeny and Bristol.

That was of course assuming that she was being

kept or had been left somewhere near her route home.   The place where her car had been discovered was the best place to start.

Freeman and Soloman reached Bodmin at one thirty am.   It had been a very long day, and tomorrow Freeman wanted to set off for Beeny at eight am.   Freeman was feeling despondent and was beginning to feel that their Superintendent would soon be demanding some answers. His low mood was passed to Soloman, and as they arrived at his flat and as he climbed wearily out of the car, it was as much as they could do to say 'goodnight' to each other.

Chapter Six

Thankfully the next day dawned sunny and bright. The temperature had dropped overnight and there was a gentle and drying breeze.

Despite the short night, Soloman was at the station at eight o'clock waiting for Freeman, who arrived fifteen minutes later, swerving to a halt.

'Sorry I am late,' he said, as Soloman got in beside him, 'my daughter is not sleeping and keeps coming into our bed.'

Soloman looked at him and noted how tired and depleted he looked. He decided then and there that today was going to be better than yesterday. Today they would achieve something positive. Today Freeman would go home proud of his

49

efforts.

The journey to Beeny was spent in silence. It seemed to Soloman that Freeman was too wrapped up in his own thoughts to do what they usually did on a car journey; they usually planned what their course of action would be on arrival. Soloman decided in his own mind that they needed to explore the area beyond the track and into the field at the end. This area had only had a cursory search, but this seemed as good as anywhere to start.

Freeman parked the car at the entrance to Gulls Retreat. They wandered through the open gate and down towards the house. Soloman seemed very keen to start on his own predetermined search across the fields, but Freeman, who was still withdrawn and sluggish, ambled across the lawn towards the French doors. The house remained locked with shutters drawn.

'Just thought I would check out the back field,' Soloman said, breaking the silence.

'I'll come with you,' the reply came back, 'it's a big area.'

Soloman strode off round the back of the house and towards the shed, hoping that Freeman would feel more energised. The sun shone and it was a very pleasant day to be outside. By the time Freeman had reached the shed, Soloman had climbed up the little steps in the wall and was over the fence within the field. There was no livestock, but judging by the freshness of the cow pats, they had been there within the last few days. He made his way carefully across the field searching here and there. His idea was to reach the far side and then walk around the perimeter. It was gently sloping and provided some shelter for the houses below. He had not gone very far before he caught sight of something sticking out of a bunch of thistles. All around, the grass had been eaten and was very short, except for this group of plants. He strode over, calling back over his shoulder, 'May have found something.'

Bending down he saw a red item of clothing, what looked like a red knitted lady's scarf. He reached into his pocket for an evidence bag. Putting on a glove, he pulled the scarf from the thistles, which had held it in place, and put it in the bag. Freeman joined him at his side and looked rather more interested.

'Well done,' he exclaimed, 'that might just give us a lead.'

They searched around for any further clues or evidence, but there appeared to be none. Three hours later, after they had looked over the whole area with no further results, they decided to leave the field.

'We should search the garden of Gulls Retreat again, and especially around the shed,' Freeman said, exerting his authority.

Soloman was pleased that he had discovered the scarf. He set off around the garden looking diligently for anything that could have been missed. They both searched, leaving nothing unturned, nothing left to chance. Sadly their efforts produced no results.

After a further two and a half hours, every area had

been inspected. They found themselves by a table in a sheltered part of the garden. It was a sun trap and even on this day late in the autumn, it was a lovely spot.

'Come on, let's have our lunch and do a summary,' Freeman said at last, just when Soloman thought that he would never be allowed to stop for a break.

'What we do have is a car, a pool of blood and a scarf, all hopefully linked to the same person, hopefully Lorretta, but where she actually is, is anyone's guess.'

Soloman was getting slightly impatient now and said firmly, 'We can rule out a hostage and ransom demand type of situation, don't you think boss?'

'Definitely,' Freeman responded, 'although there seems to be money within this family. I think that we are now, very sadly, looking for a body.'

'Better get this scarf to the forensic team, there seems to be a stain on it, maybe it's more blood, and if it is the same as we found in the shed on the first evening, then we can be fairly certain that the body started off in the field and then ended up in the shed. Why it was in the field and then the shed we don't know yet. Once analysed, we will get it up to Bristol and see if Anabella recognises it as belonging to her daughter.'

Despite its breakthrough, Freeman still seemed rather aloof on their journey home. Perhaps he is just over tired, Soloman thought. With a young baby and sleepless nights, I guess it is not surprising.

Chapter Seven

Debbie and Andrew Garrod had met at Bristol University. Having both graduated, they married and eventually settled in Bath. Debbie was a doctor in the local community and Andrew had his own architect's practice. To achieve a break away from these hectic careers they had bought a small cottage on a back lane set on a gentle green slope above Tintagel, overlooking the sea. Like many outsiders who moved into the area, they had extensively modernised and extended the property. Although they had no children of their own, the house was now capable of accommodating their extended family and friends.

Lorretta Ford had met Debbie at University. They had completed their training together and remained firm friends. Debbie and Andrew were godparents to Peter and Luke. As such the Fords had become frequent users of the Garrods' holiday home, sometimes with them and sometimes on their own.

Due to what had become a hectic week, Freeman and Soloman had not found time to speak with the Garrods until the Thursday, and despite mounting paperwork, they felt compelled to visit them before the Friday meeting with their superintendent.

At eight am Freeman and Soloman set off for Bath. Mr and Dr Garrod had agreed to meet them at their home late morning, so it was with haste that they drove north east up the motorway and out of Cornwall. It was a calm and dry day and their progress was good. Thankfully the Garrods' home was only a short distance off the main road and they arrived just before eleven o'clock.

Two new Mercedes coupes, with sequential personalised number plates were parked on the drive. The houses in this road were set back, large and individual with character.

Freeman and Soloman were greeted at the door by Mr Garrod who led them into his study at the back of the house overlooking a small and pretty garden. Dr Garrod entered and offered them a drink and ten minutes later they were all sat with coffee. Mr and Dr Garrod were both dressed in business suits and looked slightly displeased that they had been asked to leave their busy schedules.

Freeman began, 'We understand that you have a holiday home near Tintagel in North Cornwall and that you are close friends with a Dr Lorretta and Matthew Ford.'

He paused for confirmation of these points. Mr

Garrod nodded and replied, 'That is so.'

'Last week the Fords stayed at your home. They left separately, Mr Ford with the two boys and then Dr Ford sometime later. However, Dr Ford appears not to have been seen since leaving. What can you tell us about this matter?'

Soloman was surprised by the complete bluntness of the revelation of the disappearance of their friend, knowing that there was the possibility that she might be dead.

Andrew looked completely aghast at his wife Debbie, who remained serene and calm.

A cool cookie here, Soloman thought, as he looked on.

'No sign of her at all?' Mr Garrod said. 'But how can this be?'

Debbie continued, 'My best friend, Lorretta, was staying at the house with her two sons and their father last week. That is correct. Although we have in the past spent time with them at the house, we didn't on this occasion. We had other commitments.'

'I see and what were those?' Freeman continued with his direct approach.

'We were both away in Zurich for the whole week, visiting my mother. She and my father moved back there several years ago, he was Swiss. Now she is on her own and having some intensive hospital treatment. She's not been well for some time. We flew back on Sunday, and had the phone call from

Matthew on Tuesday, after he had alerted the police. He knew we were away. I think he was just checking to see if Lorretta had been in touch after Sunday, but we have not heard a word from her.'

'We will need access to your phones and proof that you were out of the country. We are extremely concerned for her well-being. We don't seem to have much in the way of any leads at the moment, and we are already four days into this case. We need as much help as possible, and to discount those that are not involved, in order that we can try to resolve her disappearance. We would like keys to the property, as it's just possible that it could hold vital clues. We also need the names and addresses of anyone who has access, such as agents, cleaners etc. Is there anyone in residence at the moment?'

The relevant names and addresses were handed over along with details of their flight and the times that they were at the airport. There was no one in the property at present and the next visitors were not due until Christmas. Keys could be collected from the cleaning lady in the village, and her address was also provided.

After handing over their own contact details and saying that they would be in touch themselves, Freeman and Soloman departed, somewhat in a hurry. There was now much to look into before first thing tomorrow.

'Call for some back up,' Freeman snapped as soon as they reached the car and set off. 'We need the team to investigate the agents while we visit the cleaner and the cottage. Get that flight checked and some kind of confirmation that they were out of the country for that period. We can't leave any stone unturned now. This is going to be another long day.'

Soloman did as he had been asked and the checks were put in motion. They traveled along in silence for a few minutes and then Soloman said, 'What did you make of those two? Do you think there is anything suspicious there?'

'I think he's alright, but she's a bit cold. We will have to keep an eye on her. Who knows what she has been up to with her best friend.'

Bright sunshine helped them on their way as they returned back towards Cornwall. Further discussions took place about the Garrods and after three hours they arrived at the top end of Boscastle, at the home of the cleaner, Tina Gambles.

Tina lived with her husband and two children in a small ex-council house. It was all she had ever known but she was content. During the summer months, Christmas, New Year and half terms, she was busy with a hectic schedule cleaning and preparing all the properties that she maintained, ready for the next holiday-makers. The Garrods had been on her books since they first arrived, and as a result they had become some of her special clients.

At this time of year, in the week following half term, her cleaning routine was reducing, and she had only been home ten minutes, having just finished the last house. She glanced out of the window at the sound of the car drawing up. She was not expecting anyone, especially two official-looking men, and wondered what they could want.

Freeman rang the doorbell and together they waited on the path by the front door. When it was eventually opened rather slowly, they were greeted by a woman, in her late thirties with long curly red hair. She had a pretty face devoid of make-up and was dressed in black leggings and a long floral 't' shirt. Despite being indoors, she was wearing walking boots.

'Good afternoon,' Soloman began, 'We are sorry to disturb you. This is DCI Freeman and I am DC Soloman.' They both held up their warrant cards.

'It's not my George, is it?' Tina said hurriedly, immediately suspecting that something had happened to her husband.
'No, no,' Soloman carried on, 'Nothing to do with your family. We just want to ask you some questions about one of your clients.'

An anxious frown swept across Tina's face.

'I haven't done anything wrong,' Tina replied, jumping to conclusions again. 'I suppose you had better come in.'

Freeman and Soloman entered and were shown into Tina's front room. It was a trifle old-fashioned but spotlessly clean. Tea was brought in on a tray and then Soloman begun his questions in earnest.

'We understand that you clean for Debbie and Andrew Garrod. Have you been to the house recently after the last guests?'

Soloman had decided to leave his questions rather

vague, in the hope that Mrs Gambles might give something away.

In a broad Cornish accent, which Soloman still found hard to understand, she answered, 'I popped in this morning just to check the place over. I shall clean it properly tomorrow.' She rattled on, 'Lorretta and Matthew are regulars. I know them personally, lovely people they are, always leave me a large bottle of gin. They leave the place spotless. She is a doctor and fanatical about the cottage being clean, so I know that I can leave it till last. Never any nasty surprises, unlike some guests. I haven't completed the change over yet. Don't expect I will have to do much any road. That any help?'

'We need to borrow the keys and have a look around. It is just as well that you have not done anything further there. Are you aware of anyone else who might have entered the property since last Sunday?'

'Mrs Deborah, as I call her, she did text me, to say that the police might want the keys. I did think it odd. She didn't say why and I just follow orders. I'm only the cleaner, so I don't know if anyone else has gone in. What's been going on there then?' She rambled on, 'nothing looked amiss to me today.'

'You won't be needed at the cottage, Mrs Gambles,' Soloman said firmly.

'It is now a possible crime scene. We will need your finger prints to start with, so that we can eliminate you from our inquiries.'

Crime scene, finger prints, elimination from

inquiries, Tina Gambles' world had suddenly turned upside down. She felt elated to be involved in something so big, nothing like this ever happened in this sleepy corner of Cornwall. Yet at the same time, she felt both confused and a little scared and worried. She led an ordinary and unexciting life filled with routines around her husband and children. Whilst everyone in the neighbourhood would want to know about Tina's new-found importance with the police, it was all rather terrifying for her. But what was the crime that had somehow embroiled her at her favourite work place, a place where she had been happy?

'So what's been going on at Rosemary Cottage?' Tina falteringly asked for a second time. She was determined to find out.

'We are investigating the apparent disappearance of one of the last guests. That, at this stage, is all we can say.'

Oh,' Tina's hand flew to her mouth. She sat down heavily, 'Those poor boys,' she said assuming that Soloman was referring to either Peter or Luke.

'That'll be it for now, give us a call if you think of anything.' Freeman said, putting his card down on the lamp table and ending the meeting. Once outside, they gathered their thoughts and then set off for Rosemary Cottage.

As they rounded a bend ten minutes later and the building came into view, they saw the vans belonging to the forensic team parked on the drive. Already the team were investigating the garden, looking for anything and everything that might help them with Lorretta's disappearance. Thankfully there was no rain, although it was forecast and the team were only hampered by the rampant shrubs and bushes which had not yet had their usual pruning.

The original part of the property was very old. It was a long white cottage that had been greatly enlarged at the rear. It was attractive with regular sash windows and a chimney at either end. A third of the way along the front was a porch, covered in long, straggly honeysuckle.

After two hours, the outside search, which included two stone outbuildings, was complete, with nothing having been found. Hopeful that the inside of the house might reveal something, they unlocked the front door and the whole team moved inside.

Soon after, it started to rain. It poured down and a few minutes later, the dismal afternoon was accompanied by thunder and lightning. The proximity of the storm was loud and intrusive. The atmosphere outside only fuelled the rather gruelling and painstaking task that was being undertaken inside. Flashes of lightning lit up the dark and cold rooms. Seconds later, the thunder crashed and rumbled as the storm moved around overhead like an angry nightmare. At one point the lightning and thunder made their presence felt simultaneously and Soloman wondered if the cottage was going to crumble around them all.

The storm had brought a darkened sky and the lights had been switched on but these flickered on and off in tune with the storm outside. The team concentrated on the task in hand. They moved first through the wide hall with its wooden staircase gently rising and then through to the drawing room with its double aspect windows. The flagstone floor in the original part of the house had been kept. Here and there bright colourful Turkish rugs broke up the monotony of the grey slate. With precision and care, everything was turned over, pulled out and checked. It was obvious that visitors had stayed at the property recently. The beds had been stripped and left airing ready for clean bedlinen. There was a large pile of washing heaped next to the machine in the utility room at the side of the house. This too was all investigated, but nothing untoward was found.

All the usual tricks known to the forensics team were used to try to detect if anything suspicious had happened at the cottage. The loft was searched, as standard practice, but nothing was revealed. Did it have secrets to impart? Soloman wondered as they all moved from room to room.

Freeman called Soloman aside. 'We had better conduct house-to-house enquiries, along this road. You take the houses up the lane and I will go down.'

At this point, Soloman knew that desperate measures were now being taken. The nearest house in either direction was at least a quarter of a mile away. It seemed very unlikely to Soloman that anybody would have been in at the exact time that something had taken place or that they would have taken note of it. But he did what had been suggested and set off on foot down the lane. Freeman took the car and drove off in the other direction to do the same.

At the cottage where Soloman knocked, an elderly lady with white hair eventually opened the door.

She had a lined and weather beaten face. A pair of bright beady eyes peered up at Soloman and a homely smell of a roast dinner followed her out. She did not appear to mind being disturbed but was unable to help. She spent all her time at the rear of her home and never knew what was happening on the road side. On most Sundays, her daughter collected her for a visit to a supermarket and then took her back for lunch and family time, at her own home. The door was firmly closed behind Soloman, who retraced his steps back to Rosemary Cottage.

The front door at the house that Freeman called at was answered by a younger woman who was accompanied by several children. Emma Watts stood in the porch and confirmed that she knew Matthew and Lorretta Ford and that her children enjoyed playing with Peter and Luke. Last Sunday, the two boys had arrived at the house first thing in the morning to say goodbye. They had spent so long promising all sorts of nonsense to each other, that their father had packed the car, said goodbye to his estranged wife and collected them en route to leaving. Little did they know or appreciate at the time that this was a perfect alibi. Emma continued by telling Freeman that Lorretta had also called two hours later when she had finished cleaning to say her goodbyes and that she would see them in the new year. She was definitely on her own. She had stood and waved goodbye, waiting while Lorretta had found a suitable driving playlist on her phone.

Freeman left the house and drove back to Rosemary Cottage. He was feeling more and more frustrated that he was no further forward with the case.

An hour later the forensic team confirmed that the house was 'clear' and that there was nothing further to investigate. They collected up their things, locked the cottage and left.

Freeman and Soloman compared notes on the drive back to Bodmin. The thunder and lightning had abated but the rain continued to fall and the roads were awash with debris. It had been another long day and both Freeman and Soloman suddenly felt very tired. Tomorrow they would have their meeting with the Superintendent. Despite all their hard work, they still had very little to go on.

Chapter Eight

On Thursday 28 October, one week before the discovery of the red scarf, Joe Branding had got up for work as usual at seven o'clock. He lived in one of the new houses at the top of Boscastle with his long term girlfriend, Cassie, and their two-year-old son, Justin. It had not been a good night. Joe had been up three times with his son, who had begun teething. It had been his turn to look after him during the night if need be, as Cassie had been on a late shift at the hospital where she was a nurse. Last night she had been on the worst shift pattern as this particular late night was immediately followed by an early start at nine am. In between finishing at ten pm and starting again in the morning, she had to travel to and from home. She could usually travel the distance in less than an hour, but last night, the main road had been closed due to a serious accident. It had taken her an extra half hour and she had arrived home even more exhausted than usual after her twelve hour shift.

Cassie had gone straight to bed, putting her head

briefly round Justin's bedroom door, where she had found Joe comforting their son, sitting on his bedside. She had seen both her 'boys' before retiring, which helped her to relax and gave her a comforting feeling, after a long day's work. Naturally she did not like to see her son in so much pain.

It was Joe's job to give Justin his breakfast, dress him and get him ready for his childcare. He had to leave at the latest by eight o'clock. Meanwhile Cassie would have more of a leisurely start before taking Justin to his baby minder on her way to the hospital.

Joe and his brother, Martin, had their own business. Primarily they did garden maintenance, but both were very versatile, and could turn their hand to decorating and general home repairs and renovations. They were well liked in the locality and respected as being conscientious and hard workers who did a good job. As a result they were busy all year round. They had built up a following of regulars, both locals and those with second and holiday homes. Generally they worked together. They had always been close, and their clients seemed to like having two brothers working on their properties.

Jean and Roger Ditchling were successful hoteliers in Poole. They had run their hotel for twenty years, taking over gradually from Jean's parents, who slowly relinquished the management and ownership to their daughter and son-in-law. They loved their life in the hospitality industry. The Palm Court was a four-star establishment and as such they aimed at a wealthier clientele. Over the years they had built up a good reputation and had much repeat business. They had a good restaurant that was also open to non-residents and here also they had picked up a good trade. They lived in a house next to the hotel and whilst being completely separate, they never felt that they could relax from the business. It was here that they had brought up their two children, Richard and Jasmine.

Richard had just finished at university and could be left to run the hotel for short periods. Jasmine was still at college but helped at the Palm Court during the holidays. It was now possible for Jean and Roger to have short periods of time to themselves and two years previously, they had purchased Tregarnon House. It had not been lived in for five years, after the previous owner, an elderly lady, had passed away. It had been neglected and was in desperate need of updating and repairs.

The Branding brothers had been introduced to Jean and Roger and had completed many of the projects both inside and out, organising and re-establishing the garden which was both overgrown and full of tired plants that had not been cared for. It had taken eighteen months to renovate the property and the grounds. Jean and Roger had been drawn to the house by the charm of this 1930 detached villa, with its sweeping lawns and sea views on the north coast of Cornwall.

Joe and Martin were still working at Tregarnon House and it was important that they finished this next part of the redevelopment plan as Martin would be away the following week visiting their mother. Joe would catch up on paperwork, sorting through their tools and equipment and completing any outstanding quotations. He might even manage to spend a little more time with his family, visiting the beach if the weather held.

He was in a good mood as he jumped into his pick-up truck and set off leaving Boscastle behind as he made his way to the Ditchlings house which lay close to Tintagel. Having lived in the locality for the past ten years he knew the twists and turns in the roads. They were narrow in places and he knew precisely where to slow down.

It was another bright and sunny morning with a low sun, but someone else did not know the road as well and took a bend a little too wide. The result was a collision between the pick-up truck and a large black estate car. It was only a very minor impact with little damage to both vehicles, but both stopped and exchanged details and insurance companies. The female driver of the black estate took responsibility. There was no way that she could not. She was over the centre of the road and driving a little too fast.

Both vehicles were drivable, and as Joe and the lady went back to their cars, Joe called out to the lady, 'I'm sure I have seen you before, is that possible?'

'No, I don't think so,' came the reply. The lady was in a hurry and not particularly concerned. Her mind seemed elsewhere. There were parking knocks, dents and scratches all over her car, despite it being fairly new. These were the kind that one associates with city living and street parking.

Joe left it at that. He was not overly concerned either. His truck was also marked at the corners and these had been caused by the endless stone walls hidden within the greenery at the road edges.

Tourists were notorious for not knowing the width of their vehicles, resulting in these minor scrapes.

When he eventually reached Tregarnon House, he told his brother what had happened, and also explained that somehow the lady looked familiar, but he simply could not place her. The brothers had a good day and almost finished the latest project: the rose garden. There was just a few hours work to finish tomorrow.

Chapter Nine

DCI Freeman and DC Soloman sat down together at Freeman's desk. They were both on their third cups of black coffee. It was the Friday morning after the body had gone missing and they had just had their weekly meeting with the superintendent, when they were required to give their boss a full update on their current caseloads. Superintendent Louise Marshall was relatively pleased with their progress, but Freeman was not happy. He hated not being further forward with the case. There were only so many hours in the day and Freeman and Soloman had been working continuously.

Their boss was realistic but at the same time, whilst quite a few relevant things had been discovered, on the surface not a great deal was happening. The detectives ran through the salient points of the case. A body had been discovered, then lost. A woman had been reported missing, by a man who lived in Manchester, who had been in the local area, and that was about it. Was there a link? If so, no one seemed to know anything about the missing woman. Why was she in Beeny? Presumably she had driven herself there and that is why her car had been found in the hamlet. Had she gone to visit someone? Someone who had subsequently left the hamlet, perhaps one of the cottage owners, or a second home owner, or someone on holiday? Instead of getting easier, the plot had thickened. The superintendent was anxious that Freeman and Soloman found answers. There had to be more.

At the meeting, the superintendent had ordered more detective constables to be assigned to the case. Two were to go to Bristol to find anything they could from Doctor Ford's colleagues. Her bank and phone records were to be more deeply investigated, which could be done from the headquarters in Bodmin. Meanwhile Freeman and Soloman were to go to the school attended by the missing woman's children, north of Bristol. Even though it was Friday, they were to set off that day and stay overnight. The owners of all the cottages in Upper Beeny were to be sought and questioned, even if this meant traveling to them, if they were second or holiday homes for rent. Superintendent Louise Marshall was adamant there had to be a link somewhere, and her team was to find it.

The boys attended a private boarding school and would still be at the school on a Saturday morning. Sometimes they remained at the school for the whole weekend, but on this occasion, they were due to be taken out by their father. Freeman dialed the school's number to arrange a time to interview the two boys. It would be useful to know how they were dealing with the fact that their mother was missing.

The telephone was answered by the school secretary. She was also the headmaster's wife and dealt with most pupil issues. She knew the boys and girls on a personal level and therefore was the ideal person to speak with. Having introduced himself, Freeman asked how Peter and Luke had taken the news about their mother's disappearance?

'We need to come and ask them some questions, and we should do so this weekend. Will the boys be at the school tomorrow?'

'The boys don't actually know yet,' came the reply. 'Their father is coming to the school first thing tomorrow to explain the situation. He is due to take them out if that seems appropriate. We are here to give full support when they come back. Peter and Luke have an important football match this afternoon, and in the scheme of things, their father felt it could wait until Saturday morning.'

'We will be there first thing at nine am to interview all three of them. If you could provide us with a suitable room, that would be most useful.'

Freeman and Soloman had an uneventful journey to the Travelodge that they had booked for that night. As they sat in the corner of the adjoining bar, away from other guests, they went over again how they would lead their meeting the following morning.

They awoke on the following day to heavy rain but managed to find their way to the school along the country lanes. It was set down a long drive and had originally been built as a small private estate.

The imposing main building of the school came into view as they rounded the last bend in the mile long drive. The main building had been built in the Victorian era and had been renovated sympathetically. There was a grand entrance porch with a big oval drive in front of it. Soloman imagined prestigious cars circling this space as the occupants were dropped off, some on a weekly basis and some daily.

Freeman parked the car in a visitor's space in front of 'The Evans Building'. Around the main grand Victorian building there were others built at different times, but at a reasoned distance away in order that the main building was not overshadowed. Whilst they were all of their era, no expense had been spared on the architecture or building materials. This was clearly an expensive school for children with wealthy parents.

It was still raining as they hurriedly made their way from the car into the main entrance via the grand porch. It was ten to nine and Soloman's eyes were wide with amazement as he looked around. Whilst he had visited many grand historical houses which opened their doors to the public, he had never been in a school such as this. Having rung the bell, they were greeted by the headmaster's wife, Abigail Braithwaite.

After the introductions, she led them a short way

down a wide passageway with its original parquet flooring and high ceiling. It was light and airy. They passed a few open doorways into classrooms. These large and spacious rooms with big bay windows overlooking immaculate lawns would have been the reception rooms of the original house. Now they were well equipped classrooms and by nine thirty they would be filled with children ready for their morning classes, even though it was a Saturday. Freeman and Soloman were shown into a smart side room furnished for visitors with a leather sofa, conference table and upright chairs. A coffee machine stood on a side board which also housed a laptop computer.

Abigail, with her perfect make up, hair, and smart business suit, looked as if she should be the Chief Executive of a successful company. Perhaps, thought Soloman, that is how a private school should be run, bearing in mind that most of the parents would be wealthy high achievers, many of whom would have their own businesses.

'Earth to Soloman,' Freeman hissed, noticing that Soloman was gazing around and studiously making a note of his surroundings, 'We have work to do, get a grip, man.'

DC Soloman recovered himself. 'Yes boss, sorry.'

Truly professional, Abigail seemed quite unfazed and continued, 'Please help yourself to coffee or tea. You can conduct your interviewing in here, please make yourselves at home. Matthew Ford has not arrived yet so the boys, Peter and Luke, don't know about their missing mother. I am sorry, I think your morning is going to be rather delayed. I have cleared my morning duties so that I am at your disposal. We can call the boys out of class at any time. We have another room like this next door which I will let Matthew use to explain the situation to his sons.'

A younger lady appeared at the door, 'Mr Ford has just arrived. I've shown him in next door. Shall I fetch the boys?'

'Thank you, Susan, that's fine, I'll go and collect them.'

Susan retreated back to her office and Abigail turned to Freeman and Soloman, 'I will try and hurry things along for you. I'll be back shortly when Matthew has told his sons.'

She closed the door and Freeman spoke. 'We're going to have to be very sensitive this morning. The boys are going to be told and then, while they are still in a shocked state, we are going to be asking them questions. This might be a very challenging time for you. Do you think you can handle it?'

There was a moment's pause while the enormity of the task sunk in.

'Yes boss, I appreciate the sensitivity required and I am ready for the challenge.'

A further twenty minutes passed and they both imagined the conversation that was happening next door. Peter and Luke would now be with their father. They would not have been expecting him until later at twelve noon. Parents could visit after the Saturday classes, watch any football matches that were being played or take their children out for the afternoon or away for one night. To be taken out of class would have left them wondering and then to be told that their mother was missing when they had only seen her less than a week ago would require great comprehension for a nine and eleven year old.

Freeman and Soloman remained silent, contemplating these thoughts as they drunk their coffee. Ten minutes later the door opened and Abigail walked in, closely followed by Matthew leading his two boys. Peter, the elder, looked pale and shaken, while Luke clasped his father's hand very tightly and had a tear-stained face.

Abigail turned to Peter and Luke, 'These are the two policemen that I told you about. They just want to ask you some questions, as we said in the other room. They understand that you are upset about the news that your father has just told you. Come and sit down over here,' she said, indicating the sofa. Her voice was soothing and calm.

Ever the professional, Soloman thought. I suppose that is what is meant by communicating at all levels.

Matthew sat down with his arms around the shoulders of each of his sons.

'Hello Peter, hello Luke,' Freeman said to each of the boys in turn, 'I am Detective Chief Inspector Freeman and this is Detective Constable Soloman. We are from Bodmin in Cornwall, not far from where you were on holiday last week.' His voice was kind and reassuring.

'When your mum did not go back to work last

Monday, your dad called us and we have been looking for her ever since. We think she might still be in Cornwall, because we found her car in Beeny near where you stayed. When you were with her last week, did you see her speaking with anyone, someone that she knew but perhaps you did not?'

The boys looked dumbfounded and a silence followed. The seconds ticked by and everyone looked at them. Eventually Luke looked up and holding on even tighter to his father's hand, he said, 'Are you a real policeman?'

 This was aimed at Freeman, and slightly bemused he responded, 'Yes, I really am, now what did you think about my question?'

Luke regained his shyness but turned away, overcome by the morning's revelations. Peter rallied and in a very grown-up voice said, 'We did not see Mum talking to anyone that we did not know.'

'What about any visitors that came to the house?'

Another silence, and then Peter spoke again, 'No, we didn't see anything, but Mum did go off on her own several times to do shopping and stuff, so we weren't with her all the time.'

'Will you think for us and if you remember anything please tell Mrs Braithwaite.' Soloman had decided it was his turn to speak.

Finally Matthew Ford spoke. 'I don't think my boys know anything but we will monitor it all and be in touch if anything comes to light. Can they go back to their classes now?'

Freeman pondered for a moment, 'Yes, no problem but we need to speak with you also, so if you could come straight back.'

Freeman spoke to Soloman once everyone had left the room.

'Just so you know, before we have a little chat with Matthew Ford, I don't think he is a suspect in the disappearance of his estranged wife. He does not seem to have motive. They have had an amicable holiday together and their boys seem sorted. There don't seem to be any financial concerns either. We need to keep him on our side, and besides I can't see how he could have done anything to his wife as he had the boys with him the whole time. They made it to their grandmother's at the correct time. Meanwhile Lorretta's car was found near where they had just had a good holiday. So we will go easy on him. No hard stuff ok?'

'Yes boss, I'm learning a lot today.'

They returned to the coffee machine and no sooner had they made themselves another cup than the door opened and Matthew Ford reappeared.

'Surprisingly, they don't seem to have taken the news too badly,' Matthew said as he too went to the coffee machine. 'I really didn't know what to expect but they are independent boys, I suppose that is one thing this school has taught them. One positive thing is that being here, rather than at home living with their mum every day, makes it a little easier on them. They have a definite routine. I don't think they saw or know anything. I can confirm that Lorretta did go off several times to do the shopping, but apart from that we were altogether.'

'Can you tell us about your friends who own the cottage where you stayed? Did you see them on your holiday?' Freeman asked.

'They are old friends of Lorretta's from her university days. She sees them quite regularly in Bristol. They live close by in Bath.'

'So what do you think happened?' Soloman asked.

'It's a complete mystery to me as well. The last time we saw her was Sunday morning, when Peter and Luke and I left. We all had breakfast together and then she stayed on to clear up at Rosemary cottage. It's always quicker and easier when the boys are not about. We left at about ten am. We may have been separated but that does not mean that I did not care for her. I wasn't expecting to speak to her again for a week or so. The first thing I knew of something being amiss was when the surgery rang to say she had not come to work for a second day running.'

'What do you know about her car being found at the end of a track, a dead end leading to fields? It was found hidden in dense undergrowth.' Soloman slid a print off from a photograph across the table to Matthew which showed the rear end of the car.

'I don't know anything about a track.'

'Do you or your ex-wife know any of the inhabitants or owners of the cottages situated either side of this track?'

79

'No, I certainly don't and Lorretta didn't to my knowledge.'

'It seems a strange place for her car to be found,' Soloman looked directly at Matthew, 'not left in a car park or at the side of a road but to all intents hidden as though we weren't to find it…..' his voice trailed off and he looked questioningly at him.

'I really don't know anything about this,' Matthew said trying to be helpful.

'Is there anything you can tell us about the neighbouring house on the other side of the cottages?' Freeman asked.

'We've driven through Beeny many times, but we don't know anyone there,' Matthew reiterated again.

Neither Freeman nor Soloman wanted to link, at this stage, the occurrence in the shed of the neighbouring house with the car found in the undergrowth several hundred metres away.

'If you think of anything, anything at all, please call us,' Freeman said with a note of desperation. He and Soloman handed over their contact details.

'That was a waste of time,' Soloman said as they walked out of the main entrance and headed towards the car. It was still raining.

'Not entirely,' Freeman responded, 'I think we've established they are all genuine with nothing to hide.'

'Better head to Bristol and see how the others are getting along with Dr Ford's colleagues.'

The rain continued and seemed to get harder the nearer to Bristol that they drove. Both Soloman and Freeman were in a low mood and the weather was not helping.

It had been a wasted trip. Nothing new had been learnt. The only positive was that Matthew could be taken off any suspect list. The time that the body was discovered in Emila's shed was about the time that Matthew was leaving Peter and Luke at their school, several hundred miles away. Unless Matthew had arranged it with someone else. Someone else who had committed the actions on Matthew's behalf. Perhaps Matthew had paid for the job to be carried out but did not know the precise details of when and how. But what would he gain and what would his motive be? They were still missing a vital link. They needed a break-through.

Solomon mused, 'Usually the killer, for that is what we are probably looking for now, would have been known to the deceased. Or was it an abductor? Perhaps the body in the shed was actually alive. Could the female body have crawled out of the shed or been taken away?'

'I don't know.' Freeman said despairingly. 'It is not getting any easier, and we have fewer leads. I really had hoped that the boys might have had something to tell us.'

Always the optimist, Soloman said, 'Perhaps something will turn up now in Bristol.'

Freeman and Soloman had arranged to meet their colleagues at the police station nearest to Clifton to have a full discussion of their findings earlier that day. Nathan Bradshaw and Sue Jones had arrived in Bristol that morning and had made their way directly to the homes of Lorretta's work colleagues.

The head receptionist, Sheila Pearson, two doctors, Jane Temple and Patrick Lincoln and the Practice Nurse, Sam Pritchard all lived relatively close to the surgery. Once they had all completely understood the importance of being interviewed in connection with the disappearance of Lorretta, they had been happy to give up their Saturday. At first, without exception, they believed that they had no information to offer the police. Lorretta was a work colleague and although she had been at the surgery for nine years, she was a private person who did not talk much about her private and home life. Her colleagues had all changed in the time she had been there and apart from day-to-day idle chat about her boys or what she was doing that evening, she shared little information.

By the time Freeman and Soloman arrived in Clifton, Bradshaw and Jones were at Sam Pritchard's flat. This was their last call. Like all the rest, they had been offered coffee or tea and most were either mid-way through their weekend chores or about to go out. Bradshaw was trying hard to be positive, as they rang the bell, despite the fact that they had achieved nothing, from their previous house calls. So far they had declined the morning beverages, but as they were invited into Sam's neat and tidy living room on the second floor, they decided to accept. Sam was trying to be as helpful as possible.

'Are you quite sure that Lorretta never mentioned anything that might be useful to our enquiry?'

What an open ended question, Sam thought. When one is having a conversation, just a little chit chat with a work colleague, one is not constantly thinking, I had better take note of this or remember that, just in case I have to answer police questions at some point later.

Sam could tell that Bradshaw and Jones were desperate for information. Finally after a moment's thought, she said, 'you mentioned that Lorretta's car had been found not far from the shed where the owner stumbled on what she thought was a body, this could infer that a local person was involved, especially as this sort of thing generally happens between people who have met before, or who have some sort of connection. I don't think she knew anyone in North Cornwall, but I do remember her telling me at a staff party we had a few years back at Christmas, she was a bit drunk, that there had been a boy once who had a crush on her, here in Bristol. I think he moved to North Cornwall, but I don't know his name or where he moved to, or even if he is still there. Not a lot of help, I'm sorry. That's all I can think of.'

'Well if you do think of anything, give us a call straight away, no matter how insignificant it might seem,' came the usual response from Bradshaw and Jones.

'No one seems to know anything about this woman,' Bradshaw said with a deep sigh as they left the flats and headed back to the Clifton police station.

83

Fifteen minutes later, Bradshaw, Jones, Freeman and Soloman were standing by the coffee machine.

'I know it is Saturday and eating into our weekends but we ought to have a pooling of information before we leave Bristol, just in case something comes to light,' Freeman said, pulling rank. 'I have just received an update, from the team in Bodmin, about Dr Ford's mobile and bank accounts. Firstly, her mobile has not been used since a week ago, last Saturday evening, when she ordered takeaway pizza. It has all checked out. The phone has not been used since. Its tracking is not on, so we can't trace its whereabouts. The bank account has not been touched either. The cards and phone are probably still in her handbag, which we have yet to find. Anyway, back to you two,' he said, turning to Bradshaw and Jones, 'Have you found anything?'

Bradshaw looked at Jones, 'Sorry boss, absolutely nothing, except a very small possibility. Our last meeting today was with the nurse Sam Pritchard, who said that at a staff Christmas party a few years ago, Lorretta told her that there had once been a boy with a crush on her who she thought may have moved to North Cornwall. It was just gossip really, almost hearsay. That's it, we don't have a name or an address, certainly not a photograph. I am just asking Bodmin to check out Lorretta's social media pages again, just in case this chap may be on there.'

At that moment Freeman's phone rang. The number did not register as someone he knew, but he answered the call, turning away from the others slightly. After a few moments listening to the caller, the others heard him say, 'We'll be round in twenty minutes.' Then turning back to the others, all he said was, 'Anabella, with some news for us, she has remembered something. That's all for now, thanks, you can call it a day.'

With that he was out of the door with Soloman hard on his heels. As they drove the short distance to Anabella's house, Soloman asked Freeman what was happening.

'She just said that she had thought of something this morning and had been pondering over its importance since. We'll have to wait and see.'

It had not been a good day for Freeman and Soloman, and now as they stood on Anabella's doorstep in the drizzling rain, they hardly felt encouraged. What was this new piece of news? They followed Anabella into her smart kitchen.

'I am so pleased that you were able to visit me, much easier to speak directly rather than try to explain on the phone. I am amazed that you were in Bristol, but then again I suppose Lorretta does live here, so you might well be here.'

Freeman and Soloman both noticed that Anabella used the present tense when referring to Lorretta.

'Yes we have been here today speaking with Lorretta's colleagues and also the boys and their father.'

Anabella pushed a plate of sandwiches towards the two policemen.

'I thought you might be hungry, coffee?'

'You're a life-saver,' Soloman said, 'I can't remember when we last ate. Coffee for me please.'

He moved towards the plate.

Anabella served the coffees and began to speak, 'Lorretta has been constantly on my mind, as you might expect. I have hardly slept, and I have been racking my brains about her friends and colleagues here in Bristol and Cornwall who might wish to harm her. She is so personable; no one has a bad word about her. I have looked on her social media pages but that is not helping; she wasn't a great one for it, just used it for Peter and Luke. But then this morning, I remembered that about fourteen years ago, around about the time she met Matthew, there was a young chap that she had met. She had a very brief fling with him; they weren't really compatible, but he developed a crush on her. She wasn't interested, but he was, and it took ages before he stopped pestering her. The important bit is that I think he may have moved further west, to Cornwall possibly. I have been trying to think of his name; I am rather stuck on Mark, but I am not sure really.'

'And you have no idea of a surname?'

'None at all, I am sorry, he just wasn't that important.'

'It is a useful point, but I am not sure that it will get us very far.' Freeman said, taking in a deep breath. He was despairing again but trying to sound grateful and positive at the same time.

'Anything else?'

Soloman noticed a slight impatience in Freeman's tone.

'Okay,' Freeman said more decisively, 'let us know if you can add to this, or if anything else comes to mind. It's time we were leaving.'

'Thanks for the sandwiches and coffee.'

'Just what is the superintendent going to say?' Freeman said two minutes later as they sat in the car pondering over the day's achievements, or lack of them. It was now raining harder again, and Freeman flicked on the wipers.

'We are still no further forward apart from this mystery lover from fourteen years ago that her mother can't remember much about.'

'We'll have a complete brainstorming session first thing on Monday and see where we go from there. Give your brain a rest tomorrow, so you can be fresh.'

Freeman could not let it rest and he continued at length, 'The trouble with this is that right at the start, no one saw another car which must have taken Lorretta away. There is obviously no CCTV in Beeny or anywhere in the vicinity. As the houses nearby are either second homes or holiday properties and they were empty, we have no witnesses, to anything. Forensics have checked the track where Lorretta's car was found, and the only thing to come to light is a red scarf found in a nearby field. I suppose we are lucky that we can tie the car and scarf together. We know that the car belongs to Lorretta Ford, the missing person.

Her phone is dead and her bank account unused. And what was her scarf doing in the field? Do you think it could have blown there from the track?'

The question was left unanswered as if it was the final straw in a very busy day where not much had been achieved.

As if to reiterate this, Soloman changed the subject and asked, 'If that is all for tonight boss, could you drop me at the railway station? It's my mother's fiftieth birthday tomorrow in Reading and I would like to be present as we have a big family party. She doesn't think I'll be coming as she knows I am working on this big case, so to surprise her would be great.'

'Sure no problem, if anything comes up tomorrow, I can cover it.'

Chapter Ten

Ten minutes later, Ore Soloman was buying a railway ticket to Reading. The next train was in thirty five minutes. Sitting on the platform with another coffee in his hand, he sent a text to his older brother, who had his own flat, near the station.

Hi Dwayne, I want to surprise Mum tomorrow. I am at Bristol now, about to get a train to Reading. Can I stay at your flat tonight? Ore

The answer came back in the affirmative. Suddenly Ore felt very tired as he sat down on the train seat. He managed to wake up after a brief nap as he reached Reading. The streets were busy with late night revelers and he was pleased to arrive at his brother's flat.

After a quick chat, catching up with each other's news, Ore eventually fell asleep. Despite spending the night on the sofa, he awoke refreshed the next day ready to greet his mother along with the other well wishers.

Ernest Soloman had taken his wife out for a birthday lunch along with the immediate family, except for Ore who as far as his mother was concerned was in Cornwall and therefore not missed. Less immediate members had been tasked with preparing the house ready for the surprise party on her return.

After an early lunch, Gladys Soloman was ready to continue her birthday celebrations at home with her immediate family. She had sandwiches to prepare and a cake to finalise with suitable decorations.

She couldn't believe her eyes when on opening the living room door, there was a shout of 'surprise' from a room full of extended family members, friends and work colleagues who had travelled from London, Swindon and Brighton. Her day was perfect. She was just beginning to think that it could not get any better, amid cheering, smiles and clapping from her guests, when there was a calm and reassuring voice behind her.

'Hello Mum.'

In an instant she knew who that voice belonged to, her beloved younger son, Ore. Try as she might, she knew it was wrong to have a favourite but for Gladys, he had always been that extra bit special.

As she turned around, the tears welled up and the emotion overwhelmed her. Ore and his mum sat down in a corner of the living room and had a long conversation. Thoughts of making sandwiches and adding decorations to a celebration cake were long gone. But that had all been taken care of by the lunchtime team.

It was a consoling chat, but at three thirty, Ore's phone rang. It was not a number that he recognised. He answered it as he was used to doing so as a policeman.

The voice at the other end sounded vaguely familiar, 'Hello this is Richard Edwards, is that DC Soloman?'

'Yes,' and after a pause, 'how can I help?'

'I am sorry to be ringing on a Sunday afternoon. You visited me last Tuesday evening enquiring about my next door neighbour. I wanted you to know that I still have not seen her or her car. Is there anymore news about her?'

'There is an ongoing investigation at the moment, and I'm afraid I can say no more about it.'

'Any chance that you could pop round later? Sorry that is a big ask, I don't even know where you are?'

Despite being in Reading with no car, and unable to add anything as far as the investigation was concerned, something urged him to say yes, he would call round.

Half an hour later, having said his goodbyes and with a tearful wave from his mother on the doorstep, he climbed into the waiting taxi and was off to the railway station. Ore's mother, saddened by his sudden departure, said that she understood. Maybe she had an instinct.

One and a half hours later, Ore Soloman was standing on Richard's doorstep, knocking. He couldn't help wondering what he was doing. There seemed to be no reason why he should be there.

Richard opened the door. He stood there smiling wearing jogging bottoms and a white 't' shirt.

Rather at a loss as to what to say, Soloman said, 'Been for a run?'

'Yes, a bit fanatical, just in and showered. I try to go every day.'

'Come in. What would you like to drink?' He said leading the way to the big open plan room at the rear of the house.

Soloman's eyes moved to the view of the small patio garden which was tastefully lit. The shutters had been closed last Tuesday. Now with them open the room seemed to flow outside.

'A coffee please.'

'Nothing stronger? I'm having a gin and tonic.'

'No that's ok, I'm fine with coffee.'

Soloman wandered over to the patio doors for a closer look outside, still wondering what he was doing in this house under the pretence of being on duty.

'There's nothing further I can add to the case at the moment,' he said, turning back to face Richard, 'unless of course you have something to tell me.'

'It's just so weird not to have seen anything of my neighbour. We don't often speak. If you and your colleague hadn't called last Tuesday, I probably wouldn't have noticed Lorretta not being about. But as you did, it adds a certain importance and now I can't stop thinking about her and where she might be.'

'Were you at anytime more than just friends with Dr Ford?'

Soloman continued in a professional manner, as he could not otherwise have asked such a personal question. He still wasn't sure why he was there. He wasn't expecting the answer he received.

'No, I most certainly was not. We were only ever good neighbours.' There was a most indignant tone in his voice but he continued more gently, 'I'm not like that.......'

His voice trailed off and there was a moment's pause. It seemed to Soloman that this correction of facts was very important to Richard.

Finally he said, 'I'm gay, we just got on really well. She arrived here soon after the break up with her husband, and we were there for each other.... as friends.'

'I see where you are coming from now.' Soloman relinquished his work mode and reacted more as a friend would.

'I am glad about that.' Richard had joined Soloman at the window and starred out into the garden. His left hand brushed his leg. 'I was rather hoping that we might be able to get to know one another a bit better.'

Soloman hadn't moved. All of a sudden a tidal wave of emotions hit him. He wasn't used to this kind of situation, and it had taken a long time for him to accept himself. For someone else to wade in so quickly and with such ease and acceptance was alien to him. He had been in this house just a week before, in a professional capacity. It was quickly becoming clear now that he was here again on a very different agenda.

'I'm very flattered, but I am in the middle of this investigation. Perhaps I could call you, and maybe later on we could meet up.'

Gone was his usual clear and precise business tone and in its place, his voice stumbled and faltered but he was so flattered. He knew, only too well, that he should not take advantage of the situation. Now as he looked at Richard, he saw him in a different light. The light brown tousled hair and the lightly tanned complexion with the blue eyes and square jaw were very appealing. Richard was the same height as Soloman and of similar build. They both had an athletic frame, and he liked what he saw.

'If you're not stopping, I'll just have to look forward to chatting with you in the meantime.'

Soloman had not had any kind of relationship before and was slightly shocked at Richard's forwardness. He pondered for a moment while he thought about the situation. Richard smiled at him. 'It'll be alright, I don't bite, well not often.' He winked. 'I suppose a hug is out of the question?'

'You suppose right. You can have something to look forward to.' Soloman smiled and taking control of the situation, 'we can chat but nothing more at the moment and now I must go and catch the last train. I have another busy day tomorrow.'

As soon as he sat down on the train seat, tiredness overwhelmed him. The last few days had been very long. He had worked hard and played hard. There had been the emotion of speaking with the Ford twins. Then there had been his mother's fiftieth birthday party, meeting family members he had not seen for a long time, the emotional reunion with his mother, and then to cap it all, someone who might be involved in his current case wanted to get to know him better on a personal level. It was all a little too much for Soloman who promptly fell asleep. Thankfully fifteen minutes before the train pulled into Bodmin Parkway, he woke up, and managed to rouse himself sufficiently to leave the train.

After a short taxi ride, he was home at last. Tomorrow was another day, or was it already tomorrow?

Chapter Eleven

The following day, Monday, the weather was typically Cornish. A wetness hung in the air. They call it mizzle. Some say it is depressing, but others try to see some beauty in this scene, for everything turns a unique grey. Many of the buildings are constructed of granite and slate. These are dotted in the countryside with fields surrounded by stone walls. The villages, towns and cities are the same, under the sky which reflects all and intensifies the landed grey. On the coastline, on such days, the sea and sky merge perfectly.

Unsurprisingly, it was Freeman who had a spring in his step that morning, in sharp contrast to Soloman. He was anxious as to how his immediate superior's mood might be. They were joined by Bradshaw and Jones in Freeman's office, coffee cups in hand.

Freeman began, 'Good morning everyone, despite all our efforts over this weekend, the only extra bit of information we have, is some vague information about a possible lover of Dr Ford's going back fourteen years. We have no photo and no name, beyond possibly 'Mark'. We need to go back to Beeny to speak with Emilia again and search the field and the lane where the car was found. Nathan and Sue, you can come with us, as you have both been assigned to the case for a few days more. Does anybody want to add anything?'

Nobody did want to add anything. The greyness from outside seemed to enter the room. After all their hard work over the weekend and in the previous week, despondency came too. A silence hung in the air as they gathered their coats and belongings. Motivation was slow coming to the team that morning.

'We better be off then,' Freeman said as he rose hastily to his feet trying to impart some energy into the others.

The others followed grudgingly.

'Do you know something that we don't?' Soloman asked Freeman.

'No, just in a good mood, Becky and I have something to celebrate, but we can talk about that later.' He beamed from ear to ear.

They made their way out to the car and set off. The mizzle was beginning to lift and a wind was picking up. They passed through the empty countryside. The only signs of life this morning were the collection of wind turbines gently turning on the top of the hill. Several were stationery, while the remainder turned slowly. Round and round, they turned, never stopping or slowing, continuous revolutions supplying electricity to the locality. It's a marvel how any electricity is created from such a slow rotation, Soloman thought randomly.

By the time that they reached Beeny, the wind had cleared the mizzle and there was a hint of sunshine, but this did little to lift the mood. Freeman parked outside the gate to Gulls Retreat and the four made their way up the drive to the house. Unlike their last visit, the house was now clearly occupied. Emilia was at home. Her car was on the drive next to a large and muddy pickup that had been hastily abandoned.

A selection of heavy duty garden tools filled the back of the truck. Soloman made it his business to peer into the interior. He wasn't sure why he was doing this. It seemed an inbuilt instinct to do so; something that had become the commonplace thing to do after his years of training. Inside was a small black backpack and a flask. A man's red hoodie top had been flung on the back seat with a towel and a pair of flip flops.

The front door was answered quickly and a smiling Emilia stood on the threshold. 'Good morning and what can I do for you? Are you any closer to discovering what happened in my shed?'

'We have made some progress, but the facts are coming to light slowly despite quite exhaustive enquiries,' Freeman answered. 'We are here today to have another look in the shed, across the field, where incidentally we found a red scarf, and in the back lane, where we also found a partly hidden car, a black Audi estate. Do you know anything about either of these?'

Emilia thought, and then as she was aware that all eyes were on her, she said, 'I can't think of anything at the moment. Why don't you do your searching and then come back for some coffee.'

'Good idea,' Soloman cut in, not wanting to be left out. He was feeling the effects of his late night.

They left Emilia on the step as they walked around the back of the house firstly into the shed where Freeman explained to Bradshaw and Jones where it was in the little stone building that the body was supposed to have lain.

'Why don't you go into the field again,' Freeman said to Soloman, when he realised that the shed was too small for them all. Freeman, Bradshaw and Jones gathered themselves inside the tiny space and Freeman was on the point of speaking when a man in his thirties arrived and stood framed in the doorway. He wore jeans and grubby boots and his white T shirt was mud and sweat stained, indicating that he had been working.

'Hello,' he said with a cheery smile, 'I am Joe Branding, Mrs Sedgewick's gardener and handyman. You here about the disappearing body? She told me all about it this morning, quite a business,' he paused and looked from one to the other, 'if I could just have the wheelbarrow and a rake, I've got to sort out the leaves, always plenty to do in a garden.'

'DCI Freeman, DS Bradshaw and Jones,' Freeman spoke, introducing himself and indicating his colleagues with a sweep of his hand. 'I think you may be able to help us. Do you know anything about a red scarf, which was found in the field up there?'

'A red scarf in the field,' he repeated as though he was being asked a complicated question. He paused...... 'No, I don't know anything about a scarf. I've never been in the field, never had a reason to.'

Freeman let the answer go without further comment and moved on to a second, 'A black Audi estate was found hidden in the bushes in the track between the cottages. Do you know anything about that?'

Joe hesitated for a moment, 'strange you should ask about an Audi, I did have a run in with a lady a week back on a bend. She was in a black Audi.'

'Go on,' Freeman said rather too firmly.

'Just that really, she came around the corner a bit too fast and struck the corner of my bumper. We got out, exchanged mobile numbers, agreed that it was just a knock and left it at that. I did take a photo of her bumper though, do you want to see it?'

The photo was found on Joe's phone and subsequently a copy sent to Freeman's mobile.

'Have you seen this lady before, here or anywhere else?'

The question seemed rather open ended to Joe, because he had partially thought he recognised her, but could not remember any further than this. He paused for a minute, and then decided that as he really could not remember, he would answer in the negative.

'No, I can't say that I have seen her before.'

'We will need to take a DNA sample and fingerprints for our records. Your finger prints and DNA will be all over this shed. Can you do those samples now, Bradshaw, got the kit in the car?'

'Right on it sir,' Bradshaw replied, and within a few moments he was back to take the samples.

'When you have finished, can you do the same with Emila? I'll go and advise her that you will be in shortly.'

When Freeman returned from the house, Bradshaw was just finishing, so he turned to Sue and asked her to take the samples from Emilia. Then turning towards Joe he asked, 'Does anyone else use this shed?'

'My brother, Martin. We work together most of the time. He would be here with me now, except that he has been delayed up country at our mother's.'

'I see,' Freeman said, 'And how long has your brother, Martin, been at your mother's?'

'I believe he went on the morning of the Sunday before yesterday.'

A week ago, Freeman thought, and without so much of a pause, he carried on, 'We had better have your mother's and Martin's addresses.'

Joe relayed them to Soloman.

'When are you expecting him back?' It was asked in an offhand manner. Freeman wished to keep the emphasis of his questioning on Joe.

'Possibly tomorrow.'

The answer was noted with a nod of the head and Freeman continued, 'Where were you, on that same Sunday between the hours of one o'clock lunchtime and ten o'clock that night?'

Joe's smile vanished as he realised the seriousness and the implications of this last question. With a look of horror, he said,

You don't think I had anything to do with this, do you?'

'Just answer the question, please.' Freeman's voice was firm and to the point.

'I was with my girlfriend, Cassie and our son, Justin, for all of that time.'

'Can you be more specific, times, places etc?'

'Yes I remember more clearly now. We, that's Cassie, Justin and myself went to Launceston, supermarket shopping late morning. We then went home and got ready for a kiddies tea party for Justin. All the parents came as well; it was a good afternoon and evening. I think the last person to leave was Gary, my mate at the garage who left about nine thirty. We all had work in the morning.'

'Right,' Freeman continued on, 'we had better take the names and addresses of everyone who came to your house with the times that they arrived and left. Set to it Bradshaw.'

Freeman was just turning on his heel to leave, when Joe interjected, 'I'm not under arrest, am I?'

'No, not at the moment, we just have to check your alibis. Perhaps it is just a coincidence that you and the missing lady bumped, literally, into one another, in your vehicles. Then two days later, a female body is discovered in this shed, which you pass through everytime you work here. In other words, the crime scene.' Freeman felt he had to make the point crystal clear. He paused, 'I'll ask you again, are you quite sure that you have never met this woman before?'

'I did say before that I had never seen her. The truth is that she did seem vaguely familiar but as I cannot remember from when or where, there seemed little point in admitting it. Maybe I was confusing her with someone else.'

Soloman saw Freeman's mood change in that instant, 'If you had admitted it at the start, it might have focused your mind. It is very important that we have all the facts,' he said angrily, 'now just think,' he ordered.

Joe's face became pale. He was an honest man who had never been in trouble with the police. He began to think but his mind was a blank under the police scrutiny. He was under no illusion now and started listing the names of their friends who had been to tea that afternoon. Bradshaw wrote them down and Freeman departed to the kitchen where Emilia was helping Sue with the DNA and finger printing tests.

Soloman appeared at Emilia's kitchen window, having given the field behind her house, the track where the car had been found and her own garden another thorough searching.

He had even spoken with the owner of the first cottage, Wayne Pickering, who was staying for the week, completing some decorating and remedial work. Although he and his family had been in residence for the half term period they had left on the Saturday evening, quite late, in order to miss the heavy traffic expected the next day.
He had been quite amazed to have heard the full story from Soloman.

It had been the same with the other owners who were staying for that week. They had all left on that Saturday evening. At Christmas and school holidays the cottages came to life as a small community. Each of the owners had got to know their neighbours. As they had tidied and cleaned their homes in preparation to leave, they had shared a picnic lunch in the track. As a result, no one had been in residence on the Sunday,

There had been a brief mention of the body in North Cornwall on the news, but Mr Pickering had not taken any notice of the news item, as it had been short and brief. The appearance of blue and white police incident tape where the Audi had been left had rather surprised him, when he had first arrived, so he had been pleased to have heard the full story from the police.

Soloman went inside and explained his findings to the others. A rather shaken Joe had been sent home, with a promise that he would be hearing from the police again if he was needed. If he was to remember anything at all, he was to telephone Freeman immediately.

Soon after, the four police officers left Emila and sat in the car to discuss the day's findings. After their discussion, as it was four o'clock it was decided that they would check out Joe Branding's alibis. They would also call at the Bodmin hospital and speak with Cassie, before visiting the supermarket in Launceston to check the CCTV to ascertain that Joe and Cassie had been there in the later part of that Sunday morning.

It was while Freeman and Soloman were driving to the supermarket that Soloman said, 'You appreciate, boss, that there is a very relevant window of opportunity for Joe, between the time of their arrival home from the supermarket to when their guests arrived for afternoon tea, roughly between one pm and three thirty pm. He never gave us an alibi for that time, and although the alibis checked out correctly so far from three thirty pm onwards we don't know what they were up to before then. We know that he was definitely at home when it was getting dark when the body was discovered and we know that the clocks had changed, meaning that it would be dark by four thirty pm or thereabouts. We should find out what he or both of them were up to in the daylight hours,' he hastily carried on for fear of Freeman squashing his ideas, 'I don't think he did it, because whoever was involved, must have been busy that evening moving the body. There is another thing, Emilia was gone for such a short time answering the telephone, twenty minutes at the most, do you think the person responsible was in the shed all the time, while Emilia was discovering it, standing at the back?'

'That thought had occurred to me a few days ago, and I was going to run it past you. I think you are probably right. Perhaps we had better discuss this with Emilia and see if she thinks it possible. After the supermarket we will go back to Boscastle and speak with the neighbours. We'll see if any of them remember seeing Joe or Cassie that afternoon before their guests arrived.'

After a lengthy wait at the supermarket while the security guard sorted through his computer, he eventually found the right day and between the three of them, they poured over the screen looking for Joe, Cassie and Justin. They appeared on the screen with Joe carrying Justin on his shoulders. The time of entry was eleven forty four am. They followed them around the store and into the coffee shop, where Cassie had a croissant and coffee and Justin helped his dad with a full English breakfast. They left the store at just before one o'clock. This fitted in exactly with the timescale that Joe had given. Freeman and Soloman were not surprised. This meant that they would be home at about one thirty pm.

Freeman and Soloman wasted no time and drove back to Boscastle as fast as the lanes permitted. It was now raining, which meant that their door-to-door enquiries would mean asking to come inside. However good fortune was with them. As they drove into the road where Joe and his family lived, the resident who lived opposite, was parking his car, having arrived home from work.

Tom Baxter lived on his own and believed that it was his duty to take note of what was happening on his estate. Anything untoward should be reported to the police. By chance, he remembered the events of the afternoon in question. He had been working an early shift that Sunday and had arrived home at two pm. Joe was washing his truck on the drive and Tom remembered a conversation with him about limited parking on new estates which always caused a potential problem for residents whenever anyone was expecting guests. Joe had ended up parking his truck on his front lawn, and then had disappeared inside only to reappear on the front door step when guests had arrived or were departing.

Mr Baxter liked to spend his spare time sitting at his front window in order to watch and take note of what was happening outside. He had been in and out of his chair all afternoon, checking on the arrivals and where the guests had eventually parked. Yes he could also confirm that Joe's truck had remained on the front lawn all evening and until the following morning when Joe had left for work. His stream of information was endless with some of what he recalled being of use. Freeman and Soloman were relieved to extricate themselves, from his constant chatter.

Freeman and Soloman called at one more house just at the entrance to the road, where again the extra vehicles entering that part of the estate on that Sunday afternoon had been noted. They had had visitors that day also and parking had been an issue for them.

They left Boscastle and returned to headquarters in Bodmin, glad in one respect that Joe appeared to be telling the truth, but at the same time disappointed that yet again they were no further ahead. It had been another long day.

'Tomorrow we will continue but for now go home and rest,' Freeman said to Soloman, as they climbed out of the car. 'Not a lot to go on, but we have a new lead to investigate, Joe's brother, Martin. His fingerprints are all over Emilia's shed, as you would expect. We need to clear him, before we go any further forward. He is due back from his mother's tomorrow. From the address we know that she lives in South Oxon near Benson. Check what vehicle is registered to Martin's address and then ask the traffic department to watch him come down the motorway to Bristol and then follow him down to Exeter. On no account do I want him to get wind of this. The traffic department must use complete discretion and unmarked cars.'

'I'll set to it first thing in the morning.' Soloman replied.

Chapter Twelve

There was still no sign of Loretta Ford – alive or dead.

Despite the fact that they were twins, Martin Branding was quite different to his brother, both in looks and in their differing outlooks on life. Once upon a time they might have looked similar, before Martin had started his regular trips to the gym. Now bodybuilding took up a large part of his life and a high proportion of his earnings.

He also had a new interest in tattoos. It had started with one, and then the addiction had turned to a stronger compulsion. It was the same with the body building. Where once it had been a keep fit and general muscle toning regime three times a week, now it was a nightly two hour session every weekday. If the business didn't need him, it was not unusual for Martin to spend a Saturday morning there as well.

Whereas Joe had settled down with Cassie, the love of his life, and started a family with the arrival of Justin, Martin had not settled. This was partly due to his bisexual nature. Despite his rather hard and aggressive look, like his brother, he had a very gentle and kind nature. He would help anyone with anything. Whereas Joe was careful with money and together with Cassie had managed to save enough for a deposit and mortgage, Martin lived in a rented flat and spent his earnings freely. They were in fact largely opposites, but this did not mean that they did not get on. They did and they managed their business very well. Martin's extra muscles came in very handy on many occasions. Both were popular in their differing spheres, Joe with the other young families, and Martin with his gym and tattoo buddies.

It was during that Monday evening that Joe decided to ring his brother. He needed to see how their mother was, check that Martin was coming back the following day and as they were twins who shared everything it was quite usual and normal for him to want to tell his brother all about his day.

All was well in Benson. Their mother had recovered from her chest infection, and Martin was all set to drive back to Cornwall the following morning and as he was going to leave early, he expected to be home at lunch-time.

The following morning on the Tuesday, the sun was shining and as Soloman walked from his flat to the Police headquarters, he was in a good mood. Yesterday there had been some developments, though not necessarily in the right direction and today, there promised to be some action with the return to Cornwall of Martin Branding and his subsequent questioning. But first he had to organise Martin's vehicle registration check. This was successful and also confirmed the state of the MOT, insurance and road tax, which were all in order.

The traffic department were contacted and all police vehicles in the area were put on a full alert for Martin and his truck. No one knew what time Martin would be setting forth and the Traffic team had to be ready and prepared. Unmarked cars would be used to follow, whilst the marked Highways Agency trucks would be observing from a distance in their lay-bys.

Martin Branding rose at six am that Tuesday. This was his usual time, though he had rested and risen later on several mornings whilst he had been away. Now he wanted to get back to his mates, the sea air and a new tattoo that he was planning. He loved his Mum and had spent the week looking after her and helping her to recuperate. At her request, they had driven out on several afternoons for a drive to a local beauty spot.

It had been good to have a call from his brother, knowing that all had gone well with the business in his absence. However, he was quite naturally a little concerned to hear about the body and that it was now missing. He had conveyed his sympathies to his brother to be passed onto Emilia, and to his brother for all the police questioning. Now it would be his turn to be questioned, but he did not have anything to be concerned about; he had been at his mother's all week.

After a breakfast of cereal and toast, and having said goodbye, Martin set off, very pleased that the sun was shining. The drive was always so much more pleasant. He had no idea, however, that so much effort had gone into monitoring his return journey.

As he reached the main roundabout where the dual carriageway met the motorway, he dithered slightly as to which direction he would take, left to Reading and London, straight ahead, or right to the south west. At the last minute, and he did not know why, he positioned himself in the left hand lane. He did not notice the unmarked police car, a silver saloon, parked on the tarmac verge. When the traffic lights changed, Martin accelerated up the slip road and onto the motorway, heading east towards Reading. He wasn't quite sure why he had done this, perhaps he just felt like it. Used to making spur-of-the-moment decisions, the police car followed, radioing in at the same time that there seemed to be a change of plan. All of a sudden, on receipt of the message, alarm bells began to ring in Freeman's head. Why the change of direction? What was he up to?

Freeman gave out the order, 'All units, change of direction. Wanted person now heading east. Follow at a discreet distance. Monitor progress and keep me informed.'

When the first exit for Reading came into view and there was no indication of Branding leaving the motorway, Freeman made a snap decision, 'Get him off at the services and question him, find out what the hell he is up to. We need him to answer questions, not spend all day cruising up the motorway.'

All in the room could sense Freeman's anger. He did not often lose his temper without justification. There was a stillness in the room as everyone waited with bated breath for what would happen next.

With sirens ringing and blue lights flashing the once inconspicuous silver police vehicle became something quite different. With Sue Jones driving and Bradshaw in the passenger seat, they soon drew level with Martin and indicated that he should pull over. They did not want to panic him and set off a full scale car chase, but they were aware of the inconsistencies of his choice of direction.

Two minutes later, after greatly increased speeds, both vehicles came to rest safely in the car park of the services. Bradshaw and Jones got out and walked quickly to the truck. A slightly bewildered Martin wound the window down, 'My brake light out, is it?'

'No sir. Could you confirm your name and address?' Jones asked quickly and directly.

Martin answered and produced his driving license.

'This is your vehicle? Where are you going today?' Jones continued.

Again Martin answered correctly but stumbled over the second part.

'I think you had better come over to the police car so we can question you.'

Sue Jones walked a few paces away and rang Freeman. Meanwhile Bradshaw settled Martin in the back of their car and began the questioning, 'We understood from your brother that you were returning home from visiting your mother. We urgently need to speak with you about a Loretta Ford who has gone missing. She was last in the shed at the home of Emilia Sedgewick, Gulls

113

Retreat, where you work from time to time. As you made as if to go towards London, we were naturally rather suspicious. Can you now tell us where you were planning to go?'

'I have an old mate in Reading, whom I was going to call on. Haven't seen him in ages.'

Sue Jones reappeared and after a few quiet words with Bradshaw, she asked Martin, 'On the Sunday before last, when you left Cornwall to visit your mother, what time did you leave?'

'I left about two pm.'

'And you drove straight to your mother's in Benson?'

'That's right.'

'Arriving at your mother's at what time?'

'Between five and six pm.'

Jones and Bradshaw got out of the car for another quiet word. After a few moments, they spoke to Martin again.

'Are you quite sure about those timings?

'Yes between five and six,' Martin reiterated.

'Those times don't tie up. We are impounding your truck for further examination and taking you back to Bodmin.'

During the time that it took for the police low-loader truck to arrive, the motorway cameras had been checked to see at what time Martin and his truck had actually passed on the Sunday before last. Eventually the report came back that Martin's truck had passed somewhat later than he had stated. The cameras at the intersection showed him passing at nineteen twenty five. If he had left his house and travelled directly to Benson, he would have been arriving at his mother's at about this time, bearing in mind the extra half term traffic. So what had he been up to in the meantime?

At around ten o'clock that morning, Detective Constable James Fisher had arrived at the home of Mrs Branding in Benson. Having identified himself, he was let in and taken through to the kitchen at the back of her terraced house. He was a quietly spoken man most suited to more sensitive cases. He was the ideal candidate for collating information.

'You have a son, Martin, I believe, who has been staying with you this last week?' James began once the offer of a coffee had been accepted and they were both seated at the table.

'Yes I do. What is all this about?'

'I just need to ascertain some dates and times concerning Martin. Your clarification will help with some ongoing enquiries.'

'No problem at all, I always like to help the police if I can,' replied Mrs Branding who was rather older in her outlook, attitude and manner than her mid-sixties might suggest.

There was a pause whilst coffee was sipped.

'Could you please tell me what time Martin arrived here on the Sunday.'

'Yes, of course. I remember that quite well, because it was much later than usual. It was after the late news, sometime between ten thirty and eleven o'clock.'

'Did he give any reason for his lateness ....as this was unusual?'

'Not really, just that he had been delayed. I didn't question him further. Didn't seem fair after he had come all this way to see his old mum. He had a bath and went more or less straight to bed. Our time together really started in the morning.'

'Did you have an enjoyable time together? When did you last see Martin? I expect you miss them both. Do you visit them in Cornwall?'

The questions and statements flowed and Mrs Branding was enjoying having this young policeman in her home brightening up her morning, or so she thought. This is where James' strength lay, in getting the best out of people by having empathy with them. By putting them at their ease, James usually found that a conversation began and information was released, sometimes unwittingly.

'That is a bit late, isn't it? You say somewhere between ten thirty and eleven?' James repeated by way of confirmation.

'Yes as I said, my dear, nearer eleven pm. I had just turned off the television. I always turn it off

116

then, just before getting into bed. I turn the bedroom light off at eleven thirty.

'I see, and you had a good week together?'

'He's a good boy, is Martin. That's not to say that Joe isn't. They are both good boys. Yes he took me out in his truck, went to the woods, it's my favourite place. I love it.'

'I'm pleased he took you out. I like walking in the woods too. Can you remember which woods?'

Mrs Branding seemed to have forgotten the reason why the young policeman was asking her questions, comfortably seated in her kitchen. It was lovely to have some company and so soon after her son had left.

'I can't remember where exactly; he knows the places that I like to walk. We park in a variety of different locations and set off from there. I think they are off the lane near the main road.'

'Can you remember which main road?' Fisher gently asked.

'The main road to Oxford, I never paid much attention, except we always went passed a big red house, with fancy gates and rhododendron bushes. I loved seeing it. We only went past when Martin took me out.'

'Did Martin ever comment on the house? Did he know who lived there?

'No he never said. There seemed to be many visitors to the house. We often had to slow to allow them to turn in or let them out.'

DC Fisher studiously wrote notes. He would compile his report and pass it to his superiors.

'Would you recognise this property? Do you know how far it is from here?'

'Fifteen minutes, or thereabouts.'

The detective constable smiled weakly at Mrs Branding. He wrote more notes but at the same time felt that he wasn't able to pursue much in the way of facts. As she did not seem to know where this house was, there would be no point in taking her out in the car to try to find it. It would be quicker to look himself. It couldn't be that far away. He would start with looking at historical houses which opened to the public. He concluded his thoughts and notes with the fact that there might not be any relevance in this red house in any case.

He smiled again and she looked back intently at him.

He closed his laptop, 'I think that answers all my questions, thank you. You have been most helpful.'

'I know what the next line is,' said a giggly Mrs Branding, 'if I think of anything else I am to phone you straight away.'

As she said this, she held her hand out, 'you are supposed to give me your details at this point.'

He handed her his card and said, 'I think you have been watching too many crime dramas.'

'I love a good crime drama,' Mrs Branding stood holding the door, not appreciating that one was unfolding in front of her.

'Thank you for the coffee,'

Half a mile down the road, James stopped the car in a layby and phoned Freeman and explained all that he had been told. This added information confirmed to Freeman that Martin's own timings were pure fiction.

Chapter 13

Martin Branding had been brought to the police headquarters for questioning and his truck had been fully investigated. There were remnants of bleach on the sides and floor of the load bed and the torn tonneau cover which were now spotless. They were too clean for a what a gardener transported.

However there were clumps of mud and wet leaves in the wheel arches and underneath, indicating that the truck had been off road. This would not seem unusual bearing in mind the rural locations that Martin visited during the course of his work. They were however tested and a mixture of soils had been found; some only to be found in Cornwall and some from South Oxon.

What was more sinister were two tiny spots of blood on the dash board, close to the air vents. Perhaps he had cut himself at some point in the past. The rest of the dashboard was unrealistically clean apart from a little recent dust. Martin was asked if he usually kept his truck in this manner. His reply was that when he had time off and visited his mum, it was his first job on arrival, in order that she would be travelling in a clean vehicle on any outings that they made.

DC Fisher had been dispatched back to speak with Mrs Branding to check on Martin's story of cleaning the truck. Yes he did usually wash it, but this time, he had seemed to be very obsessive, asking for bleach and cleaning clothes. None of the latter she had seen again, but Martin had promised to buy replacements when he took her shopping. That first morning he had used so many buckets of hot water washing the interior, that the hot tank had run dry, something which had never happened before. This was after he had been to the local car wash at the nearby supermarket first thing before breakfast and before his mother was up. At the time Mrs Branding had thought it all rather strange but had quickly dismissed her worries. She concluded that her son only wanted the best for his mum.

Freeman called a meeting with Soloman, Bradshaw and Jones. Branding was in an interview room next door. A police officer stood guard at the door.

'Here is a summary of our findings with Martin Branding,' Freeman started, 'Although he seems an honest man in his daily life, well respected and liked in his community, with no police history or previous questioning, with a good business with his brother, who speaks highly of him as does his mother, there are now rather too many flaws in his otherwise quite plausible story of recent events. He is a man in his thirties who has not been in any trouble before. It is quite likely that we have the answer to our case here. I think that whatever has happened has been unintentional. A long series of mistakes have been made. Martin Branding must be questioned on his differing time scales as to why he was so much later arriving at his mother's. Are we all agreed that there is nothing else to add here, before we formally question him? I propose that Soloman leads the interview, it will be good practice for you.' He turned to Soloman for an acknowledgement.

'I'll be pleased to boss.'

Freeman continued, 'Despite the seriousness of this crime, I don't believe Branding is a hardened criminal, so I suggest a gentle approach. In fact I insist. I think we will achieve more that way.'

Everyone agreed and Soloman made his way to the interview room. Freeman followed and Bradshaw and Jones watched proceedings through one-way glass in the adjoining room.

Chapter 14

Ore Soloman felt reasonably confident in what Freeman had asked him to do. It was not his first case where he had been the main interviewer. But this was the first time he had been dealing with such a serious and potentially high profile case. He did not have much time to do his final preparations. It was true that he had been involved right from the beginning. A gentle approach, Soloman said to himself over and over again as he walked the few paces from the meeting room to the interview room.

The usual police interview proceedings took place with the introductions and the start of the recording.

Soloman began, 'Mr Branding, do you understand why you are here?'

There was a pause, while Martin looked at his solicitor for guidance. There was an acknowledgment from his solicitor, who was a slim and petite lady in her late twenties. Despite her comparatively young years, she had a hardened look about her, which implied that she had experienced many different cases. Joe had managed to find her, on a good recommendation from a friend. Her smart and precise appearance gave a good impression, one of complete efficiency and surety. She nodded as if giving the go ahead of a predetermined plan of action.

'No comment,' Martin eventually replied. He hung his head down low, and his words were barely audible.

'Can you speak louder please, for the tape,' Soloman replied.

Freeman sighed heavily. Not this route, he thought, we have wasted enough time already.

'No comment,' again came the reply, this time it was just loud enough.

Soloman continued, 'Had you met Lorretta Ford before the date in question?'

He was determined to get the ball rolling; there had to be a starting point. It was in some respects like watching a tennis match, Soloman versus Branding. The tension was the same. When would Branding start to cooperate and answer questions? Or would Freeman have to intercept and takeover?

There was a lengthy pause. It wasn't as if Martin was thinking about his answer. His head remained low, covered by his hands. He was a broken man. Finally, after a further gentle prompt from Soloman, the answer came back as before.

'No comment.'

'I have advised my client not to comment,' the young solicitor interrupted the tennis sequence. There was almost a slight menace in her tone, but Soloman was not put off. His last training course had dealt with this same situation.

After a few more questions regarding Martin Branding's earlier life in Bristol, which had all received the no comment response, Soloman decided to take a different approach. Perhaps if he made an assumption or two in his questioning, he might break the no comment rally. This was just as well, as Freeman's sighs had been getting more and more pronounced. He was about to intervene when something told him to wait. He had given this opportunity to Soloman and now he should allow his questioning to continue.

'Martin,' Soloman's voice was calm and gentle, 'did you find yourself in the garden shed at Gulls Retreat, with Lorretta Ford on the evening in question?'

Soloman had decided that perhaps a better approach would be to ask a non-suggestive question regarding the whereabouts of Lorretta Ford. There was the now customary pause, while Martin gathered himself. It felt like an eternity. All eyes were on him.

'I'm not a bad man,' he stuttered, 'It all went so wrong.'

Soloman was a little taken aback.

'When I saw her, I just wanted her to notice me and remember the good times that we had before.'

Somehow the voice and the words that were coming out, did not quite fit with this big, strong, tattooed bodybuilder.

'I am not sure that we quite follow, perhaps we could start at the beginning as in when you first met Lorretta.'

Despite the fact that Soloman knew that the victim more often than not knew or had some connection with his or her assailant, Freeman and the rest of the team had not considered fully that there might be a long term past connection here. All enquiries into her past had drawn a blank, except for that vague mention by Lorretta's mother about a former boyfriend, who she thought had moved west and whose name she believed had begun with M, possibly Mark. It was not much to go on.

'I first met Lorretta about sixteen years ago, and I fell in love with her straight away. I worked at the big hospital in Bristol as a porter in the Emergency department. Lorretta was a junior doctor doing her training. We were both very young, early twenties. I thought she was wonderful, but of course she was out of my league.'

Martin Branding paused, and his whole upper body fell forward. With his head resting on the table edge in front of him, gentle sobs rose from his chest. Soloman was pleased that he had been guided towards a gentle approach. A hard line was more often than not what was called for, but in this instance it would have been wrong.

'Please go on.' Soloman said, appreciating that this was difficult for Branding and yet at the same time not wishing him to stop.

'We did go out a few times, and at first I thought we would be able to have a future together. We were only kids. But after about six months, she told me that we were finished. I was gutted, my whole life just dropped away. About six months later, I think she met someone else, whom she married. She finished her training and left the hospital. I imagine she became a GP somewhere. I had moved to the maintenance team at the hospital, by this time. Shortly afterwards, my brother and I decided that we were getting nowhere in the big city and decided to move to Cornwall for an easier life. We thought we would enjoy getting into the surfing scene.'

He seemed to rally a little at this stage, as though the thought of those early halcyon days of starting a new life somewhere more relaxed had momentarily taken the edge off the current situation.

'I had not seen or heard from her until a week ago last Saturday. It was her voice that I remembered, and then the face clicked. She was just coming out of a shop in Boscastle with two young boys. And then it all came back. I assumed that there was a husband around the corner somewhere, and I didn't want to cause any trouble. It really got me thinking. That could have been me with my own family.'

The sobs had finished and he lifted his head from the table. A little smile passed across his face as if he was remembering the good times all those years ago.
Soloman and the solicitor took a breath. Freeman

sat patiently at the side, pleased that information was forthcoming. There was a pause in the proceedings. But Soloman did not need to encourage, for Martin continued, as if wanting to get it all off his chest.

'I tried not to think about her that evening. I didn't think I would see her again and I wish I hadn't. But on the Sunday, before I left for my mum's, I had promised a mate that I would look at a possible future job near Boscastle, at a big farm. I was pulling out of the gate when who should drive past, but Lorretta. It all came back to me. I followed her up the road, flashing my lights and sounding the horn. She seemed in a hurry. She was in the car on her own.'

The sobbing started again.

'All I wanted was to have a chat, make sure she was alright. Eventually she pulled in where the cottages are in Beeny. I was so pleased, but then........' he faltered. 'It all went terribly wrong. I followed her up the track. She had parked at the end, I got out and she did too. I went towards her but she was furious. Furious that I had made her stop. She must have thought I was some sort of madman. Then she recognised me but one sort of fear overtook the first, a fear of a stalking boyfriend whom she had ditched years ago. In her haste she failed to put the handbrake on when she got out, and her car rolled forward into the bushes. I had blocked her in, in her mind, so she set off up the track and over the gate. All I wanted was a quick chat.'

The sobbing was in full force now, so Soloman allowed a pause. He wondered what the others

128

were making of this story behind the one-way glass.

'I called out that I only wanted a chat, see how she was, but she carried on running across the field. And then it happened. She was nearly at the end of the field, but she tripped on a rock in the ground and came down really hard on the stone wall at the end. When I got to her, she was out cold. But of course I couldn't leave her. It was beginning to rain. She had a nasty cut on her head which was bleeding profusely. All I could think of was to get her inside, so I picked her up and carried her back down the field. It was raining very hard by the time we got to the fence by Emilia's, I just wanted to get inside the shed. I was going to ask Emilia to ring for an ambulance....'

There was another pause, while Martin wiped his face, and drew breath.

'Take a moment's pause and a drink of water,' Soloman said gently. 'You're doing very well.'

'It was getting dark. I laid Lorretta down on the floor very gently. At least it was dry in there. I had just put my sweatshirt under her head, and was about to go to the back door, when I heard footsteps. I panicked completely. My head was not thinking. But I did not want to alarm Emilia or scare her. It was one thing to knock on her door to ask for an ambulance. Quite another to be found in her shed in the dark with an unconscious body asking for her help. How would I explain that? So I stood right back in the little recess by the work bench and hoped that she didn't come in. But she did and then the worst thing, she tripped up over Lorretta. I completely panicked then. I had to get away, but I

129

could not leave Lorretta there, so as soon as Emilia left, I carried her to my truck and laid her very gently on the load bed. I was very gentle with her I promise.'

Sensing the need for a kind gesture, Soloman added, 'I am sure you were.'

'I drove without stopping, with my dear Loretta in the back, all the way to my mum's.'

It now seemed that Martin Branding had taken on a child-like manner as if during the course of his monologue he had reverted back to his younger days.

'And where is Lorretta now?' Soloman asked hoping that he could finally get to the bottom of this case and know the full story.

Emotion now took a hold of Martin Branding. He looked at Soloman and then Freeman. There were tears in his eyes which ran down his cheeks. It was as if he had told his story and then his brain and memory had seized, overwrought by the enormity of the facts.

They remained in the room for a further ten minutes, but Martin Branding refused to say anything further. He had drawn a veil over the whereabouts of Lorretta. Freeman attempted to coax more information from him but it was all to no avail. All they could ascertain was that Lorretta was no longer alive and that she was buried somewhere in South Oxon.

Martin Brandon's solicitor advised the two policemen that they were not going to find out anymore that day. Her client had been very helpful. Branding was exhausted and after a slow start he had been helpful and forthcoming in his account of what had happened. Sadly they still did not know where Lorretta lay, but at least Martin had admitted to the fact of letting Lorretta die in the back of his pick-up truck on the way to Benson. He also admitted to burying her body, but he either genuinely could not remember where or he refused to say.

Martin Branding was charged with manslaughter and kept in custody until the trial, which was set for the following springtime. He refused to say anything more about Lorretta.

That evening, at Freeman's request, the four of them and the superintendent met at the local pub, The Pirate Ship, for celebratory drinks. Louise Marshall was pleased, saying that the original few clues had made it a difficult case. Thankfully it had been resolved quickly once they had brought in Martin Branding.

Both Freeman and Soloman were due leave.

When asked what he was going to do, he replied, 'I am spending time with my wife and daughter in the Lake District with my sister. She has a wonderful house overlooking Lake Windemere. We are going to have some quality family catch up time and,' he paused beaming from ear to ear, 'Becky, my wife is pregnant.'

They all cheered and congratulated Freeman.

'Have a wonderful time with your sister and family,' Soloman added.

They all turned to Soloman, was he happy? Had he made the right choice to leave Reading? Yes, all was good and how was he going to spend his time off? Drawing a deep breath, he said. 'I am off to Bristol to spend a few days with Richard.'

They all looked blank.

'Who is Richard?' Louise Marshall asked.

'I have been chatting with Richard Edwards over the last few evenings and we have decided that it would be good to spend some time together.'

There was a continued look of uncertainty between them, so Soloman clarified, 'You remember Richard Edwards. He lives next door to where Loretta Ford lived.'

'Good for you mate,' Bradshaw said, 'Sorry we didn't know, we hope it goes well for you.'

Smiling, Ore concluded with, 'If I play my cards right, I might be applying for a transfer to Bristol!'

In early March the following year, at the Truro law courts, the judge acknowledged that Martin Branding was a man of previous excellent character, who had made a terrible mistake. He had wasted police time, by not coming forward at the time, but had been forthcoming during his interview, which had held him in good stead. However, he simply refused to give any hint as to where Lorretta's body lay. For these reasons he was given a ten year sentence.

Chapter 15

It had been a very wet January and February at the start of the following year. Martha Tickling and Tilly had not been able to go out for their usual walks on the heath. This had upset Tilly far more than Martha. Tilly was a delightful apricot Yorkshire Terrier. She and Martha were devoted to each other. Tilly was a very pretty dog, who loved her walks, even if it was raining and the ground underfoot was sodden and muddy. Martha was in her early sixties and although fit and sprightly she did not share Tilly's enthusiasm for 'wet walks'. She was happy to take her but perhaps on days, when it was raining, not quite as far as Tilly would have liked.

They had a variety of routes, near the cottage where they lived. Tilly usually chose. There were even some that required the use of the car as they were further afield. It was quite usual for them to spend two hours walking in the morning with a shorter route in the evening.

On that particular morning in early March, after the heavy rains the night before, Tilly was in her element, trotting along, 'reading' the doggy signs and enjoying all the extra smells and scents that the rain had left. Martha was treading a little more warily. Her wellington boots were not the best footwear for traversing a muddy slope down the edge of a field. Martha always let Tilly off her lead at the top gate. She knew her way, and would scamper ahead quite happily, under the gate and into the woods beyond. Not so poor Martha, she had nearly slipped over twice already, and although she was happy for Tilly to go ahead, she did prefer to be able to see her.

But on this morning, Tilly was away and into the woods along an overgrown path. It had very little use due to its inaccessibility. As it was still early and the sun was shining weakly, there was hope for a better day. Suddenly, Martha heard barking a way off in the distance. It was most unusual for Tilly to bark especially with this consistency. Martha walked as quickly as she could in the circumstances. She slipped several times, but just managed to stop herself from falling. What on earth could be the cause of all this? Martha thought. Tilly seemed to have gone off the tiny path and was deep in the undergrowth. It was most unlike her.

If she had not known her pet as well as she did, Martha might not have bothered pushing herself forward through the wet branches and brambles. She consoled herself that with it being winter, there were far less wet leaves on the bushes, and she had more chance of seeing where she was putting her feet. None of this had troubled Tilly who had simply scampered underneath the low branches. Eventually having followed the incessant barking for what seemed an age, she saw Tilly ahead.

Calling and reassuring her made no difference and the barking continued on unabated. Martha consoled herself that she could at least see her now. At first she saw nothing out of the ordinary, just her dear Tilly barking by a pile of leaves. They were now on the side of a slope, in a little clearing.

Unbeknown to Martha, they were only a short distance from a more popular path on the other side where the bank rose up again. As she drew close, she could see that the recent heavy rain had washed the leaves and soil away. To her horror she saw that Tilly was barking at a human hand that was sticking out of the ground. Martha felt a wave of nausea creep over her and as she half sat down and half fell, she managed to find her phone, in her pocket, praying that there would be a signal. Thankfully there was and having called for the police, she and Tilly sat a short distance away and waited for them. Tilly took quite some consoling while they waited for what seemed like hours.

After the body had been exhumed from its shallow grave and the tests had been done, Martha was eventually informed that the body was that of a Dr Lorretta Ford who had been missing since the previous October. She had been on holiday in Cornwall at the time of her disappearance, a well-liked GP from the Clifton area of Bristol.

Martin Branding remained completely emotionless when he was told, overcome by the torment of what he had done.

Today Martha and Tilly are a little older and less able to manage such strenuous walks. If you should see them, they will probably be walking in a more public space.

****

I hope that you have enjoyed this book. If you would like to follow DCI Freeman and DC Soloman as they investigate more cases, you may wish to read 'No Panic' and 'No Fear'.

No Panic

When the parents of Simon and Vanessa fail to return from holidaying in Cornwall, investigations begin. It's a long hot scorching summer, and the West Country is even busier than usual with extra visitors. But when two persons mysteriously disappear without trace, no one is prepared for the dark secrets that are uncovered. Police officers Freeman and Soloman start to unravel the case amidst great changes in their own personal lives.

No Fear

It is February and a body is found at the bottom of a cliff on the north Cornwall coast. Detectives Freeman and Soloman start to unravel the ensuing mystery. A few months later, a second mysterious death occurs connected to the same family, in similar circumstances, 1600 miles away. Freeman and Soloman rush to help the local police, as more complications unfold. The plot winds around developments in their own personal lives, causing heartache and complications for the two detectives.

Are the two deaths connected, or is it just a coincidence?

Printed in Great Britain
by Amazon

68909855R00090